Maid to Serve

The Lesbian Billionaire

Claire Kirkland

ISBN 9798357433091

CONTENTS

The Heart Wants

PROLOGUE

Leslie chuckled as her billionaire boss gazed at the blonde inside the coffee shop. Cassandra Cardona owned five mansions on three continents, two yachts, and enough cars to drive a different exotic every week. And yet, she displayed no confidence as her fingers clutched the Louis Vuitton purse instead of the door handle of the Ferrari.

"Nervous?" Leslie gently punched Cassandra, who treated her as a friend rather than an employee.

"I feel like I'm making the same mistake," Cassandra said. She didn't face Leslie when she spoke, still staring at the oblivious girl at the table.

"It doesn't have to be a mistake." Leslie put her hand on Cassandra's arm. "Just because Linda—"

"Don't say her name." Cassandra glanced at Leslie, showing a hint of kindness that made up for her snarl. Leslie understood her wealthy friend, even if she disagreed with her approach.

Though Cassandra paid dozens of young women to fill her enormous mansion, she had always been explicit about the arrangement being one of friendship. Except for Linda. Cassandra had chosen her to be her lover, only to end up falling for her. But Linda drew the line at a friends-with-benefits relationship. When Cassandra desired more of her, the servant ran off. Since then, Cassandra grew lonelier, which she only admitted when Leslie pressed the matter. Making friends as a billionaire proved challenging enough—finding a girlfriend seemed impossible. She didn't trust any woman's interest in her, fearing they were out for her riches.

Cassandra still had her needs, however, so she had tasked one of her servants to find her a new lover. She vowed to keep things strictly sexual this time around. Leslie knew better. Cassandra's dreamy eyes told her everything. Miranda, who had found the perfect girlfriend for Cassandra, wanted to make a bet with Leslie, but they shared the same expectation—Cassandra would fall for Nina Mayfield within days.

"All right," Cassandra sighed as she opened the door. "It's a simple offer. I'm sure she'll take it."

"I'm not worried about her," Leslie said. "But you're not being honest with yourself."

Cassandra glared, though it had no effect on Leslie. They had been close for so long that Leslie saw through the bratty attitude.

"I don't want to fall in love again," Cassandra mumbled while getting out of the red supercar.

As her boss entered the coffee shop, Leslie shook her head. "Oh, but you will."

A Wish Granted

CHAPTER 1

"I would make a great housewife," Nina said to her best friend. "I just need to find a rich girl to take me in, that's all."

Hope sipped her coffee before nodding at the lady in the white dress who just sat down a few tables away from them. "Like her?"

The brunette in the classy dress had her back toward them. Nina looked at her without a care. *Yes, like her.* She appeared to be in her early twenties, like Nina, but that's where the similarities ended. The lady's neat, shiny hair reached to her butt, and her soft, tan skin shone in the morning sunlight. Her fashion showed a mix of elegance and youthfulness. Even her posture screamed upper class. *No, not upper class. Far above it.*

When the barista approached her, the posh lady glanced up at her with an air of superiority. Nina got a little tingly watching the resting bitch face, with her pouty lips and narrowed eyes. It's as if the barista spoiled the woman's mood by daring to address her.

"You're staring," Hope said. She wasn't wrong, but Nina couldn't look away. The woman caught her attention in a way nobody else did. The server smiled wryly and bowed her head a little. Nina imagined herself in the barista's place. *Yes, miss. I'll get your order right away, miss.* Most people Nina knew loathed entitled brats, but it turned her on when a confident woman took charge. And yet, she somehow always attracted girls who were like her— shy, withdrawn, and submissive. It led to short, un-eventful relationships…on the rare occasion she even stuck around after a first date. This brunette, how-ever, seemed to be what Nina craved, even if she concluded that after mere seconds of admiring the woman.

"Still staring." Hope kicked Nina's leg under the table. "You are desperate, aren't you?"

Nina glared at her friend. Just because it was the truth, didn't mean Hope had the right to call her out like that. She took her empty coffee mug with trem-bling hands to hold on to something.

"All jokes aside," Nina said, "I am in deep shit."

Peering back over her shoulder again, Nina had to force herself to stop being so awkward. Hope rolled her eyes and said, "Hey, it sucks that you couldn't make it through college, but there are plenty of jobs in this economy."

She pointed her thumb at the barista passing them by. Nina sighed. *She has a point.* Almost every business in town had recruitment signs at the en-trances, begging for people to work for them. Some even offered hefty bonuses. These small towns couldn't keep people from leaving for the big cities. It made Nina wonder what the gorgeous, mysterious woman behind her was all about. She seemed out of place here, with earrings and armbands that probably cost more than Hope's monthly salary. Perhaps even her annual income.

"Take a job here, right here." Hope tapped a finger on the table. "The pay isn't great, but at least you'll have an income."

Hope wanted the best for Nina, even when the troubled girl didn't bother to get her life back on track. Hope already offered a place in her tiny apartment, despite it being barely large enough for herself. But being told her grades weren't good enough to stay in college killed Nina's motivation to do any work. Not that she even wanted any of those bigshot careers. Her indifference and lack of a goal no doubt played a big part in her flunking out of college. She didn't see herself serving coffee all day, either.

As the barista returned with a coffee for the stunning woman, Nina followed her with her eyes. She caught the brunette glancing her way as well, and Nina dropped her gaze. Just a split second of eye contact was enough to bring her down. Those deep brown eyes claimed her heart already.

"No wonder you're single, Nini," Hope said. "Whenever you fall for a girl like that, you're too afraid to even say hi."

Nina looked outside, avoiding her friend's taunting smile—and the nickname. Nina had long since stopped correcting Hope, even if she hated how childish it sounded. "This is different."

"Why? Because she's Cassandra Cardona?"

Nina's eyes snapped to her friend. "Wait, you know her?"

Hope snorted. "You don't?"

Nina took another peek at the brunette. She had turned away again and read something on her phone —the latest and most expensive, of course. Her purse was more expensive than all the clothes Nina wore—although the college dropout prided herself in picking complete outfits for less than one hundred dollars. Her pink halter top cost less than the coffee, thanks to a fantastic discount. She still got by on financial support from her parents, who she hadn't yet informed of her status as an unemployed, uneducated woman with no plans. But as much as they cared for her, Nina didn't want to move back in with them.

The gorgeous lady, who Hope somehow knew of, turned her head ever so slightly, and the corner of her pretty mouth curled into a sly smile. Her name, Cassandra Cardona, didn't ring a bell for Nina. *Should it?* Nina asked Hope who this woman was.

"You've seriously never heard of her?" Hope frowned. "She's, like, literally your type. Bitchy twenty-four-year-old billionaire with a history of getting sued by former staff…and lovers. Often both. She's right up your alley."

Nina's eyes widened. "Sued? What for?"

Hope savored her coffee rather than answering, knowing how to tease 'Nini' so well. When she put the mug down, Hope leaned forward as if she shared a deep secret. "She's known to be…rough."

"Rough?" Nina leaned in as well. "Be specific!"

Hope took her phone and, after half a minute of tapping and swiping, showed Nina the screen. Nina's jaw dropped at the sight of the photo of a perky blonde with bright eyes—who looked eerily like her. The headline under the picture made her heart flutter.

"Cass choked me when I didn't lick her ass," the woman had admitted in the interview. Nina read the first few lines of the article, which made it clear miss Cardona had a way of demanding a lot of depravity from her employee. Nina couldn't believe her eyes.

As if she could read minds, Hope lounged back and said, "You're such a slut. You'd love her for doing that, wouldn't you?"

"Don't judge me," Nina lowered my head. "But…I guess she's hiring now?"

Her heart skipped a beat when the angelic voice behind her answered. "Yes, pet, I am."

Hope stared at her with an open mouth, fighting the urge to laugh as Nina froze in place. Nina didn't dare move, even as Cassandra's pretty legs came into view. *How did she even hear us? She was like ten feet away!*

Her heart raced, and time slowed down to a crawl. When Cassandra's slender, manicured fingers reached for her chin, Nina held her breath. Cassandra touched her—gripped her—and she almost cooed. Cassandra forced Nina to look up. *What an absolute goddess.* Cassandra's predatory grin shrunk what little confidence Nina had, but it made the butterflies in her stomach even wilder. *Nobody should be this beautiful.*

"You think you have what it takes to serve me?" Cassandra turned Nina's head to the left and then to the right as if she were inspecting a product. But Nina didn't stop her. Shy as she was, she knew her worth as a woman. She wasn't as voluptuous as Hope, or as tall as Cassandra, but her curves drew in plenty of attention. And if Cassandra's recent employee was any indication, Nina was as much Cassandra's type as the other way around. Well, perhaps not quite the same. Nina had never seen this woman online, but she had a hard time imagining the rich lady looking even prettier with filters. The expertly applied makeup helped, of course, but it appeared to enhance her natural beauty rather than mask her true self.

"You're allowed to answer me," Cassandra said, snapping Nina out of her daydream. The words didn't even sound like a tease—Cassandra seemed vain enough to mean it.

"I'm sorry," Nina said, her voice but a whisper. She didn't even know why she apologized, but it felt like the right thing to do. Cassandra's soft laugh confirmed she made the right choice.

"Good girl." Cassandra ran her thumb over Nina's cheek. Nina panted as she gazed up, and she only vaguely realized how crazy she looked. But if there was even a remote chance of Cassandra being serious, Nina had to take it. She just didn't know how to tell her. Her voice caught in her throat as she tried to speak.

"You're so cute." Cassandra played with Nina's bottom lip. "But I'm not sure if you can handle serving me."

Whatever happened, Hope would never let her forget this moment—so she reasoned there was no harm in going all the way. She swallowed, working up the courage to answer.

"I'm willing to try," Nina said. "If you'll let me."

Cassandra still held her chin and smiled. Nina wasn't sure if the expression showed a strange affection—or possession. Either way worked for her.

"Prove it." Cassandra narrowed her eyes and let Nina go. "Show me what you can do in the restroom."

Nina nearly fainted at hearing the offer, especially with Cassandra's casual tone. Staring in awe, Cassandra had Nina speechless once again. But she knew she could put her mouth to better use than speaking...she just had to get up and walk. And yet, she didn't. She looked at Cassandra like a puppy waiting to be guided.

"Well?" Cassandra put her hands at her side and cocked her head. "You're not all show, are you?"

In Nina's mind, she was already in the restroom, kneeling on the cold tiles and worshiping Cassandra's divine body. She had no objections—no shame —to submitting to the brat. In fact, she desired it. But yearning for something and doing it were two different things—and Nina was too shy to act on her needs.

"You have until I finish my coffee," Cassandra said. "If you're not in the restroom by then, I'll find someone better. Perhaps your pretty friend here."

"Fuck off," Hope snarled, never afraid to lash out. "Besides, she'll be there."

Hope's voice of confidence warmed Nina's heart, but she still had to prove her friend right. Cassandra walked away, and Nina gazed at her until she sat down. Cassandra focused on her phone again and didn't so much as glance back at the conflicted girl, pretending as if the conversation never even happened. *Perhaps it hadn't.* Nina's mind still spun. *I'll wake up any moment now.* She looked back at Hope, whose expression was a mix of surprise and a bit of disgust.

"You'll do it, won't you?" Hope shook her head. "I mean, she'll probably compensate you well, but..."

"But?"

"She might be right about you. I'm unsure if you can survive having her as your boss."

Offended, Nina crossed her arms. "What is that supposed to mean?"

"Look at her," Hope said. "You think you can be lazy around her? No offense, but I don't think you're disciplined enough for her."

"I'll prove you wrong!" Nina got up from her seat, suddenly finding herself standing when she feared her body wouldn't listen. With the first step taken, the motivation to walk away from her table and toward the toilets came easy. She forced herself not to glance at Cassandra as she passed her and rushed into the restroom with a heightened pulse.

Assessment

CHAPTER 2

Is this really happening? Nina looked at herself in the mirror. Her fierce blush made her look exactly how she felt—shy, naughty, and oh so willing. A growing part of her feared that Cassandra and Hope were pulling a prank. After all, Nina had never heard of the supposedly famous billionaire. *Billionaire. That's a lot of money.* Cassandra could just be one of Hope's friends, the two of them waiting outside to tease Nina about falling for this nonsense.

When the door opened, Cassandra's stern face washed away Nina's worries...and reinforced her anxiety. The brunette had the natural expression of an entitled brat. Nina moved back, but Cassandra closed the distance and grabbed Nina's shoulders. Before she could react, Nina got pushed into the stall, getting dangerously intimate with the bossy brat.

With Cassandra's legs spread and her hands pressing down on Nina's shoulders, the instructions were clear. The joy of finding employment in Cassandra's mansion didn't compare to the kinky desire to go down on the gorgeous stranger in the restroom of a coffee shop. Nina's shy attitude always clashed with her wild desires, but now she had found someone willing to take her the way she wanted.

Nina dropped to her knees onto the cold floor without breaking eye contact—Cassandra was too beautiful not to gaze at. The lower Nina went, the more natural her place became. Cassandra already owned her. One of her hands stroked Nina's blonde hair while the other lifted the summer dress. As much as Nina desired to stare at the brunette's pretty face, the lure between her legs became too strong.

The tiny white thong enticed Nina to take the next step. The sheer fabric hinted at the beauty Cassandra offered, and Nina inched forward to kiss her lips. Cassandra purred as her prey submitted. Without the courage to speak, Nina made sure her mouth proved her devotion in a better way. *Take me home. I'll do anything for you.* She kissed Cassandra's thigh—tasting a hint of sweat—and licked her vulva through her thong.

Cassandra hiked her tight dress up a little higher and took Nina's head with both hands. "Take my panties off."

She didn't need to tell the submissive blonde twice. Nina slid the thong down her lover's legs, giving both of them exactly what they wanted. Cassandra's eagerness showed with a hint of wetness on her lips. Nina lapped it up dutifully. In itself, the flavor didn't impress more than other women, but the novelty of submitting in a public restroom had Nina's head spinning.

Taking it slow enough to savor the moment, she kissed and licked Cassandra's pussy without diving in or tending to her clit. She would either have to force Nina or wait for her to proceed—and Nina much preferred the former. Cassandra's dress wrapped tightly around her waist, fitting her form so well it had to be tailored to her. She stared down at Nina with an indifferent expression, but her thighs jerked when her lover licked her slit. Nina fluttered her eyes before kissing Cassandra's lips firmly, marking her with pretty pink lipstick.

"Is this the best you can do?" Cassandra's fingers ran through Nina's hair and pulled her in. She needed it just like that—to be controlled. Cassandra angled her hips and pressed Nina's face into her cunt, forcing herself on Nina just the way the submissive girl desired. Nina moaned into her lover's pussy. She didn't fake it. Cassandra's labia engulfing Nina's mouth and nose had her licking the delightful, wet pussy with devotion.

Nina's exes and flings had always been too passive and careful. Only a few of them tried sitting on her face or spanking her, but they would stop every few seconds in worry. Cassandra didn't seem like that type. When Nina playfully denied her and tried to withdraw her tongue, Cassandra's vagina tightened—as did her grip on Nina's head. She slid back and forth before Nina could submit again, using her nose as a little toy to stimulate her clit.

To prove she was worth it, Nina fought the hold on her to wiggle up and kiss Cassandra's clit, wrapping her lips over the little button and flicking her tongue rapidly. Cassandra's yelp sent little jolts down to Nina's core. Satisfying the stranger shouldn't bring Nina such pride, but she struggled not to sink her fingers into her panties. She forced herself to dedicate her attention to her purpose—and her queen.

"Don't stop." Cassandra's thumbs stroked Nina's head. "Keep doing that with your tongue."

Her voice lacked grace now, and it spurred Nina on. She smiled as she stared at the tiny patch of hair above Cassandra's mound, her heart fluttering with pride as she debased herself for the rich brat. As she licked and kissed Cassandra's clit, the lewd squelching filled the tiny room with delightful proof of her desire, while Nina's mind filled with questions. *Did she come here looking for a new servant? Was the barista her first choice? Could I really become a live-in maid for a bratty billionaire?*

All the unknowns swam around in Nina's brain while her mouth worked on instinct. As Cassandra's juices coated her chin, Nina lowered to French kiss her lover again. Cassandra's hands tugged at her hair, demanding her elsewhere, but she needed to drink her love.

"Get back on my clit," Cassandra hissed, but Nina couldn't bring herself to pull her tongue out of the tight vagina. She wiggled around inside, drawing out more of Cassandra's wetness while the domme's grip turned painful.

Cassandra finally yanked her away, hard. Nina didn't get the chance to admire her lover's gorgeous face. Cassandra slapped Nina's cheek and forced her back on her clit. Nina's head spun with shameful desire—the burning sensation in her cheek surged down to her pussy. *She slapped me!* Nina almost tried pulling away to thank Cassandra for it.

Even when Nina begged her lovers to do it, none of them ever struck her during sex. And yet, Cassandra didn't even hesitate, stinging Nina's cheek without care.

Nina assaulted Cassandra's clit with doting kisses and frantic licks, giving her what she desired and demanded. Cassandra also yearned for something much rougher than Nina was used to. Even as Cassandra's thighs trembled and her moans cracked, she urged Nina to go on. "Faster! Harder!"

Nina's pulse raced, and she gave her lover one last push. Nibbling Cassandra's clit broke her resistance and sent her over the edge. Her thighs clamped down on Nina's cheeks. She screamed, crying out a long "fuck" that seemed below her station. But here in the restroom, Cassandra was no billionaire brat. Here, she surrendered to her wanton needs—riding Nina's face with jerky motions and drenching her in her love. Nina didn't relent. She used every moment Cassandra gave her to suck her clit as if her life depended on it, keeping Cassandra's voice pitched high until she moaned deeply and pushed Nina back.

"Oh, fuck, enough..." Cassandra brought her hand to Nina's forehead to stop her from diving back in. Cassandra's other hand stroked Nina's hair, making a mess of it. Nina didn't care about how she looked—only the approval of her lover mattered. The giggling confirmed that without a doubt. Nina caught her breath as she stared at her boss-to-be, holding her hands together to stop the urge to finger herself.

Kneeling for the amazing lady, with that cute voice and stern face, excited Nina beyond her wildest dreams. Cassandra's desires aligned perfectly with Nina's. Cassandra needed a willing slut who she could ride to orgasm without care. Nina needed to *be* that slut. She arched her back a little to present herself as the eager submissive.

When Cassandra opened her eyes and looked down, Nina almost lost the willpower to not masturbate. Those brown eyes drew her in, refusing to let her go, while the entitled grin showed Cassandra's true nature. She got off on making women do this, but that didn't scare Nina one bit. These selfish desires were the one thing she looked for in a woman, and Cassandra's whole life centered on that.

Cassandra pulled her thong back up to cover her mound, but the way her excitement soaked the sheer underwear was a reward of its own for Nina. The lewd display proved unbearable. She had to keep herself from leaning back in to lick the flimsy fabric. Cassandra grabbed Nina's chin and pulled her back to her feet.

Nina wanted to kiss her lover. She almost leaned in, but Cassandra's stern expression made it all too clear she didn't have that privilege. She promised herself to perform so well that one day, Cassandra would be the one to surrender. Maybe Hope believed Nina lacked discipline, but Nina would do anything for Cassandra.

Cassandra spun Nina around and put her hand on the small of Nina's back, casually guiding her out of the stall. Her reflection startled her—ravaged and slutty. Cassandra didn't let her freshen up. Cassandra put her arm around Nina's waist and dragged her out, back into the public area.

Nina would have frozen up again if it weren't for Cassandra taking control. She played with the edge of her white pants and looked down at the floor, awaiting whatever was required of her. Cassandra reached into her purse, which she had left unattended on the couch without care, pulling out a pen that was probably worth more than Nina's car.

"You've earned yourself a chance." Cassandra scribbled something on a napkin. "Report to Leslie at my home. Don't bother bringing anything. You'll have everything you want when you live with me."

The Tour

CHAPTER 3

Nina had taken Cassandra's napkin with shaking hands. *She wasn't kidding.* Nina earned herself a job and a place to live, all because she eagerly licked Cassandra's pussy...which she would have done for free.

Without so much as a goodbye, let alone a kiss, Cassandra had taken her purse and strutted away. The young woman was the very definition of an ice queen. No sane person would subject herself to such a twisted relationship—but Nina didn't mind being insane. Not if it meant free housing, a job, and the opportunity to taste that amazing woman again.

Hope put down her phone when Nina sat back down at the table. Nina could barely look her friend in the eye, but when she did, Hope laughed hard enough to startle the passing barista.

"Oh, fuck," Hope said. "you're such a whore."

"You're the one who convinced me to do it." Nina tried to fix her hair in vain.

"Bullshit. You were drooling over her. But...was it worth it?"

Nina showed the napkin with a shit-eating grin on her face. "I've got the job!"

"I always knew you had a talented tongue, Nini." Hope grabbed her phone and took a photo before Nina could object. She didn't even mind. If she should have been ashamed, she sure as hell wasn't.

A bright red convertible pulled out of the parking lot, with Nina's new boss in the passenger seat. Nina smiled at what she had somehow accomplished. Twenty minutes ago, she was an unemployed disappointment. Now, she had a future that promised so much more than just money and a roof over her head.

"For what it's worth," Hope said, "I'm happy for you. It's weird as shit, but if you can make it work..."

"Oh, I will make it work!" Nina put her hands on the table. "I have to."

"Just be careful." Hope took Nina's hands. "I wasn't kidding about how rough she is. Please, be careful."

Nina smiled and nodded. Hope always looked after her. Nina agreed to have another coffee before chasing after Cassandra, convinced by her best friend not to be too desperate. If that was even possible after giving herself to the wealthy brat within moments of meeting her. Hope couldn't distract Nina from the ever-increasing presence Cassandra claimed in her dirty mind. Nina apologized for her absentmindedness and kissed her friend goodbye before leaving the coffee shop in a hurry.

NINA'S OLD, CREAKY SEDAN didn't do well on long trips, banging and wobbling along, but she soon wouldn't have to worry about the costs of gas and maintenance anymore. While Cassandra hadn't mentioned a wage or work hours, Nina trusted the compensation would be satisfying enough. Along with the prospect of living under the billionaire's roof, Nina needed no more convincing.

The address Cassandra gave her led Nina on a one-hour drive into the middle of nowhere, her mind occupied with all sorts of kinky scenarios the gorgeous brunette had in store. She thought about the article Hope showed her. The former employee refused to lick Cassandra's ass, which Nina found absurd. *Who wouldn't want to worship that?*

The last few miles of the journey didn't require navigation. There was only one house in sight, located right at the edge of a large lake. In all her years of living in the area, Nina never came out this way. It was a perfect private location, with just a single road leading in and out. Cassandra's wealth became more and more obvious. The size of her mansion seemed absurd for one person, and so did the helicopter—on a platform larger than the house of Nina's parents.

A short but bulky brown woman in a form-fitting black outfit raised her hand, ordering Nina to stop. She came up to the window, but Nina waved at her to take a step back. "Window's stuck!"

Nina opened the door and frowned at the woman holding her right hand near a holster. *Armed guards? Jesus. She's not playing around.* She looked at the woman's face and felt a little anxious. As proud as she was of her somewhat stereotypical blonde hair and blue eyes, the exotic woman melted Nina's heart almost as much as Cassandra did. It wasn't just the pretty face. The tight outfit left little to the imagination—her absurd tits and ass made her look like a porn star. *A very strong porn star.*

"Turn back around, girl." The woman nodded toward the long road. "There's nothing for you here."

"I'm Nina Mayfield. I'm here for Cassandra," Nina said.

The dark beauty stared her down with a hint of disgust. "Miss Cardona doesn't want to see you."

Nina gulped. *Like hell she doesn't.*

"She invited me," Nina said, failing to sound confident. "She hired me."

"You?" The guard raised her nose as if Nina insulted her mother. "You're not worthy to clean her boots."

Ignoring the fact she was armed and muscular, Nina got out of the car and said, "I'll gladly clean her boots! But I guess you're just jealous she hired *me* to be her servant."

Nina didn't know what came over her. Picking a fight wasn't like her, but she hated how smug this little bitch was. Worse, she couldn't stand the thought of the sexy, dark woman being allowed near Cassandra instead of her.

"Good, you have spirit." The thick guard stepped up. Even though Nina had to glance down to meet her gaze, the guard stared Nina down like she could crush her in a heartbeat. If Cassandra hadn't already claimed it, Nina's heart would beat faster for the feisty woman. The guard winked at Nina. "You'll need that fire if you want to make it."

Nina relaxed a little, now that the threat had disappeared. The little taunts put her on edge, but she told herself to stop being so defensive over Cassandra. Clearly, the billionaire didn't need her protection.

"Go on, get in there." The brown girl shook her head with a smile—no doubt at seeing Nina's dreamy expression. She opened the gate with a remote, and Nina hurried back into her car as the thick guard walked into the compound.

Nina drove down the enormous courtyard, spotting a red Ferrari. She could only imagine how expensive—and exclusive—it was. Its aggressive shape matched Cassandra's attitude. Nina parked her rust bucket between the Ferrari and another exotic, chuckling as she realized the wheels probably cost more than her scratched and dented car. She got out and walked around her simple sedan to inspect the other outrageous car. The navy blue sports car somehow looked less aggressive, yet more imposing. She didn't recognize the shield-like logo, and she figured it was so exclusive it justified her ignorance.

Another young woman approached while the pretty guard strolled down to the backyard, which was about as big as a football field. Cassandra's choice of staff had a pattern to it—she seemed to only employ gorgeous girls. This one, blonde like Nina, wore a white bikini that fit her perfectly, even if it was too tiny. Her long ponytail swayed along with her hips. Nina's gut wrenched when she pictured Cassandra choosing the bikini blonde over her. *Stop it. Cassandra chose you.* The host flashed a broad smile and nodded at the car.

"Beauty, isn't it?" She ran her hand over the side of the car as if it were a horse. "A Koenigsegg."

"A what kind of egg?" Nina frowned at the gibberish coming from the girl's mouth.

The bikini blonde's laugh was warm rather than demeaning. She tapped her phone, and Nina stepped back as the enormous doors of the supercar slid out and upward. Nina's nostrils flared at the sight. *That's just showing off for the sake of it.*

"Not a fan of exotics?" The girl closed the doors again with a single tap. She waved toward the entrance of the immense mansion. "Let me show you around, then. There's something here for everyone."

Nina followed the pretty girl inside. The foyer alone dwarfed her parents' home, garden included. Cassandra's choice of art made her interests pretty clear. A huge painting of a sapphic orgy loomed over one doorway, and Nina stopped to admire it. Whoever created it had a dirty mind, and Nina wondered if Cassandra ever re-enacted the scene with her staff. These thoughts worried her as much as they excited her. She wouldn't mind being part of an all-girl orgy...but she couldn't bear the idea of Cassandra favoring another woman.

The host turned around and smiled.

"That piece always draws attention." She leaned in a little too close for Nina's liking. "I'm Leslie, by the way."

"Nina," she mumbled without looking at Leslie. Serving Cassandra was easy—meeting her hot servants wasn't. But Nina didn't resist when Leslie took her hand, dragging her toward the kitchen. One of the kitchens, at least.

"You're not expected to make breakfast for Cass." Leslie stopped and looked Nina right in the eyes. "But you'll eat her pussy when she eats her meal."

Nina gulped. Not because the blunt statement rattled her…but because she was eager for the opportunity. Cassandra's essence still lingered on her lips, and that didn't shame her. If her other duties allowed it, Nina planned to seek recipes and cooking lessons to serve Cassandra the best meals—even if it wasn't required. *I'll be her best servant yet!*

Leslie smiled at Nina's determined expression. "Good. You're not bothered by that at all, are you?"

"She asked me to lick her in the restroom of a coffee shop," Nina said, trying to sound as casual as possible. "I know why I'm here."

Leslie winked. "Yeah, that's how she tested your predecessor as well. But she still ran off…"

Nina's heart sank. The more she listened to the other girl, the more her confidence shrunk. *Maybe I was arrogant to think I'm special.* Knowing Cassandra had dozens of gorgeous girls here made Nina fear for her chances.

"Hey, don't be down." Leslie ran her hand down Nina's arm. "She picked you for a reason. If you're as ready to be dirty as you say, you'll be fine."

Leslie guided the newcomer to the large windows overlooking the gardens. "And you get a lot in return, too."

Nina sighed at the attempt to soothe her. All of this seemed too good to be true. Even if the other girl abhorred the idea of licking Cassandra's butt, leaving all of this behind was a lot to give up—even in the name of dignity.

"Does she ask the same of you? Like, all her staff?" Nina asked. She needed to know what she was up against.

Leslie smiled. "Cass keeps us around because she's lonely. It's difficult making friends as a billionaire, apparently. But…"

"But?"

Leslie put her hands on Nina's shoulders. "As far as I know, she's loyal—if she chooses you."

Nina frowned. "You're telling me she doesn't play with any of you hotties?"

Leslie shook her head as she took Nina's hand and guided the girl into the next room—a dimly lit lounge with rows of bookshelves. Nina wondered if the billionaire even read. Perhaps she just needed to fill the place up with more than just sexy women.

"Cassandra has demanded nothing sexually of me." Leslie dragged Nina through a hallway and into a—relatively—small cinema. "I'm here because I love cars. And Tess, for example, often goes horse riding with her. Everyone here has something Cass likes about them. As friends."

Leslie held Nina's hand as she explained it. Nina's jealousy made way for amazement. She couldn't fathom how Cassandra kept away from Leslie and her incredible figure, especially since she liked blondes…and paid for Leslie's presence.

"She may be a handful," Leslie stroked Nina's arms, "but she's not a maniac. I don't know if she'll want more from you than just your tongue, though."

The brazen comment caught Nina off guard. "What do you mean?"

"Come on. If she wants to be monogamous to her sex slave, do you really think that's all she desires?"

Nina's heart fluttered at the thought. Submitting to Cassandra made her dreams come true, but Leslie suggested the possibility of more. A relationship with the billionaire? Nina couldn't see it, not with how bratty Cassandra was...and yet, the idea intrigued her.

"I'm just saying." Leslie walked Nina down a new hallway. "Linda might not have left because of the sex, but Cass' desire for more."

"Well," Nina said. "I'm willing to give it a shot. All of it."

"I hope so. Cass deserves to find love."

The rest of the tour proved less eventful, but the casual nature of being guided through the maze of wealth reinforced the oddity of knowing Nina had access to it all—if she agreed to serve Cassandra. A shiver ran down Nina's spine as she considered the crazy arrangement. *I can't wait to tell Hope about this!*

Proving Herself

CHAPTER 4

"And this is you." Leslie threw the double doors wide open. Nina's jaw dropped. She shoved her guide aside to step into the room—her room. The bed alone would take up half of the dorm room she was used to, and the place was all tidied up like the most luxurious of hotels.

Leslie laughed while Nina admired the place with held breath, feeling the fabric of the curtains and trailing the makeup table with her fingers. Leslie winked as she opened another door, revealing a bathroom with a jacuzzi—and a window in the ceiling. The blue sky lit up the bathroom in a calm, natural glow. Nina stepped inside, staring up at the sky above.

"I can't believe it," Nina said. "I'm going to lounge in here every day."

By now, Nina had gotten used to Leslie's touch a little and even leaned back against her when her arms ran down Nina's side.

"I think you'll spend more time elsewhere," Leslie giggled, "if you're so eager to please Cass."

Nina broke away, only to ask if Leslie could show her Cassandra's bedroom.

"Not so fast." Leslie jerked Nina back while she already started to leave. "You need to get changed first."

Nina stopped in her tracks, facing Leslie with a grin. *Of course.* Cassandra deserved the best, and she no doubt had a lot of expensive attires for her.

Leslie opened the walk-in closet, or rather, a whole changing room almost as big as the bedroom itself. The wardrobe held more clothes than Nina had owned in all her life, with dozens of dresses, lingerie sets, and bikinis. She took out a swimsuit. *Just my size...?*

"Leslie? Why is this exactly my fit?" Nina held out the pretty one-piece and approached her host. "That can't be a coincidence."

Leslie clapped her hands like a child. "Finally! You're figuring it out, aren't you?"

Nina frowned and cocked her head. Leslie's reaction only confused her more.

"Come on, Nina." Leslie dropped her shoulders in defeat. "You didn't think it was a little strange that a filthy rich billionaire just showed up out of nowhere to offer you this life?"

Nina shrugged. *Kind of?*

"We all have a purpose here." Leslie slipped the straps of Nina's pink shirt down her shoulders. Nina didn't even think about stopping her. "Miranda is a brilliant designer, but also Cassandra's scout."

Nina took Leslie's hands as the eager girl tried to take off Nina's top. "That explains nothing. How does she know my measurements? Or that I'd even agree to this?"

"She's good at what she does." Leslie tugged on Nina's shirt until she relented. "Honestly, she scares me with how good she is at stalking people."

"I don't understand." Nina covered her now naked tits with her arms.

Despite her earlier, near-inappropriate attention, Leslie made no sexual move now. She pointed at Nina's pants while she browsed through the range of outfits. Nina sat down on the soft bench in the middle of the changing room to take her pants off as instructed.

"Miranda works at the boutique in town," Leslie said. "You know, the one called Miranda's."

Now it made sense to Nina. At least, somewhat. That store specialized in affordable but tailored underwear. Did Cassandra pay Miranda to look out for specific girls—poor and pretty? The woman's lingerie didn't exactly fit Cassandra's status. Leslie didn't give her a chance to ask the million other questions that came up as she tossed her a black satin outfit with light frills.

"I'M GLAD YOU'RE FINDING YOUR PLACE." Cassandra's voice startled Nina. Leslie seemed unfazed as she compared a few pairs of heels, but Cassandra's eyes focused solely on Nina.

Nina felt no shame as she stood naked before her, and said, "I'm very glad to be here, miss."

Cassandra beamed. "Such manners! I'm impressed."

Nina blushed at the compliment. This was her life now—making Cassandra happy. She didn't mind that prospect one bit.

"I take it Leslie has given you the lay of the land?" Cassandra caressed Nina's cheek. She closed her eyes, surrendering to the gentle touch.

"Mostly," Nina said. "It'll take days to see everything here."

Cassandra's warm laugh clashed with her earlier coldness at the coffee shop. Perhaps she relaxed now that she knew Nina belonged to her. She winked at Leslie, prickling Nina's heart with some envy. Nina stood still, awkwardly awaiting what came next.

"Thank you for welcoming her," Cassandra said to Leslie, who smiled back.

"Of course, Cass." Leslie rubbed Nina's bare shoulder before stepping away. "Have fun, girls."

Cassandra turned to Nina, who didn't dare break away from her gaze. "So...do you still want to serve me?"

"Yes!" Nina stepped forward as she answered without hesitation. "I'm yours, any way you want me!"

Leslie laughed as she hurried out of the room, giving the lovers much-needed privacy. Cassandra teased by inching closer with her gorgeous lips, but she shoved Nina back when the girl fell into her trap and moved in for a kiss. Nina stumbled against the low couch.

"Are you sure?" Cassandra emphasized her words with a glare. "Once you're in—"

"I'm sure!" Nina jumped up and got right in front of Cassandra. She didn't know how Miranda figured out she was Cassandra's type, but she wasn't shy about her desires. Especially with Leslie's hint at a romantic future. Nina trembled with adrenaline, praying her eagerness didn't appear rude.

"You're delicate." Cassandra cupped Nina's tits and ran her thumbs over her nipples. The slight touch was enough to make Nina moan. She wasn't prepared for the slap across her cheek, let alone the way Cassandra spat on her face right after. Nina yelped, but she didn't so much as raise her hands. As disgraceful as it was, feeling Cassandra's saliva dribble down her cheek relit the fire in her pussy.

"I'm not weak," Nina whispered. "I can handle you."

She wiped Cassandra's spit from her face and couldn't help but lick it up to prove her devotion. She yearned for more of the rich girl, even if she was stuck-up, rough, and nasty.

"Prove it." Cassandra briefly rubbed Nina's pussy before shoving her down to her knees. That slight touch alone made her swoon.

Cassandra stared down at her for the second time this morning, and Nina licked her lips in anticipation. Cassandra held her chin again, the same way she did before, but now Nina saw the slap coming and braced for it. She didn't jerk back or complain, even though it stung and made her eyes water. The greater challenge was keeping her hands away from her pussy.

With Cassandra's arousal still—or again—strong in the air, the lure of her treasure became hard to ignore. But Nina kept herself fixated on the bitchy face and blinked through the tears. Cassandra caressed Nina where she had slapped her, then twirled around on her feet and glanced back. "Lick my ass, Nina."

Cassandra's command fulfilled Nina's wish. She had never done it before, but she couldn't think of a better woman to be her first. The naughtiness of kissing Cassandra's asshole before ever kissing her mouth was an incredible, sinful encouragement. Cassandra didn't lift her dress. She let Nina do all the work now. If Linda's reason to leave truly was this barrier, Nina had a bright future ahead of her.

As she inched forward on the plush carpet, Nina appreciated how lucky she was. While her predecessor saw this as a limit, getting to serve a bratty domme only struck her as a perk on its own. She tried not to seem too desperate, but perhaps it was already too late for that. Her hands trembled as she reached for Cassandra's dress, but she kept herself from diving in right away. She held on to the thin fabric and kissed the back of Cassandra's thighs.

Cassandra giggled, driving Nina to repeat it and take it slow. They had all the time in the world now, and she would only stop if her legs gave out. So close to her treasure, Nina had to fight the urge to just kiss those soaked panties again, but she devoted her mouth to peppering Cassandra's mighty thighs with her love. Cassandra failed to maintain her highness when Nina swiftly moved up and smooched her cheeks.

Her toned butt appeared big enough under the tight dress, but having it bare and right up in Nina's face overwhelmed her. She squeezed Cassandra's butt and licked it all over, showing her love without words—and receiving the same through Cassandra's moans.

Bratty as she was, Cassandra appreciated a slow submission. She didn't force or command Nina to speed up. But Nina lacked that discipline. Worshiping the billionaire while naked on her knees proved too much. She prayed Cassandra wouldn't notice—or care—that she slipped one hand between her thighs, gently seeking her pussy while her tongue pleased Cassandra.

Nina kept the thong in place for now and wiggled her face between Cassandra's cheeks, kissing her pucker—covered only by a thin white strap of cotton. Cassandra giggled and spread her cheeks, and Nina licked all of her ass without shame. Her fingers moved on their own, working their way inside her pussy, wet and willing as it was. Cassandra had Nina on edge from the moment they met. Now that she prepared to tongue-fuck Cassandra's asshole, it became a struggle to hold back her high.

"Come on, pet." Cassandra wiggled against Nina's face. "Show me how much you want me."

With some effort, Nina withdrew her fingers from her pussy to pull down Cassandra's drenched thong with both hands. Her rosebud enthralled Nina, even if a quiet voice of hesitation cautioned her. *What if I don't like it?* Cassandra inched back, pressing her asshole right against Nina's mouth, removing all worry and hesitation. Nina kissed firmly, submitting in full.

"Good girl!" Cassandra pressed back even more. Nina held on to her thighs, embracing her role. She lapped over Cassandra's pucker, flexing her tongue as she did before in Cassandra's pussy. Nina's heart fluttered as she poked against another woman's ass for the first time in her life. Cassandra's muscles gave way to the firm pressure, welcoming Nina's tongue as it sank into her ass.

The lewd embrace made Cassandra moan even deeper, driving Nina to play with her pussy again. She slid two fingers inside with eager need while rubbing her clit in circles with her other hand. The squelching as she fingered herself was far from subtle

—Cassandra laughed even as Nina wiggled her tongue deeper.

"You're such a slut." Cassandra leaned back, practically sitting on Nina's face. "You're gonna come for me with your tongue in my asshole, aren't you?"

Nina moaned a resounding "yes" into her lover's ass, with her lips pressed right over Cassandra's asshole and her tongue wiggling deeper inside. She curled her fingers inside her cunt to rub her G-spot. The novelty of slathering her tongue deep in Cassandra's ass made her head spin. She gave up her dignity to make out with Cassandra's asshole like a dirty slut. Spurred on by complete submission, Nina moved her hand to Cassandra's thighs, leaving her dripping pussy yearning for a touch.

"Oh..." Cassandra's legs twitched when Nina caressed her labia. "All right..."

Nina smiled with her mouth on Cassandra's ass, enjoying how her actions surprised her lover. If this was the moment of truth, Nina swore to impress. Cassandra welcomed the already slick fingers into her tender vagina, and her sphincter caressed Nina's tongue the deeper it went.

Nina picked up the pace, sliding in and out of Cassandra's pussy as delightful squishing filled her ears—along with hushed whimpers. Nina wrapped her other arm around Cassandra's hips and sought her clit, working her with the same fervor that made her come not so long ago.

"Fuck, Nina!" Cassandra took Nina's head with both hands and pressed down, just the way Nina wanted. "Deeper!"

While her tongue had no more to give, Nina twisted her fingers and finger-banged Cassandra so hard she feared it became too much—but Cassandra spurred Nina on while singing her name. The sound of the filthy billionaire losing herself nearly put Nina over the edge. With her hands occupied, she pressed her thighs together in need. Cassandra took a third finger with ease, while Nina frantically kissed her asshole, fighting the spasming muscles. At the risk of going too far, Nina slapped Cassandra's clit.

"Nyaa!" Cassandra arched herself on Nina's face, smothering her whole, while her ass and pussy clamped around the invading tongue and fingers. Nina fought against it, spearing her tongue just a little deeper as Cassandra worked to expel her. One of Cassandra's hands shot to Nina's, but she ignored Cassandra's grip and rubbed her clit between her index and ring fingers, drawing out heart-warming moans.

Nina rode out the thrill as best she could. Cassandra yanked away her hand, but Nina twirled her tongue even wilder while rubbing the sensitive spot in Cassandra's vagina. Cassandra cried in joy. Her legs trembled, and Nina only relented when she feared her lover would collapse. Even then, she withdrew her tongue slower than her fingers, savoring the tightness of Cassandra's asshole.

When she slipped away, finally, Nina licked her fingers without thinking while lowering her other hand to her pussy.

"No, no," Cassandra turned and gave Nina a correcting tap on the nose. "That's enough, pet."

Nina whimpered and pouted, but Cassandra's sexual high already made way for the bitchy face—even if her eyes glowed with pure pleasure. She played a game and Nina suffered for it. But as close as she was to her orgasm, Nina obeyed and put her hands on her thighs like a good girl.

"You're something else, aren't you?" Cassandra asked.

Feeling a little brave, Nina shrugged and said, "I keep trying to tell you. I'll be the best servant you've ever had."

Cassandra stroked Nina's cheek. The slight touch filled her with warmth and hope. Every second Cassandra let her prove it, Nina came that much closer to securing her position. It had been mere hours since they met, but Nina already desired more of Cassandra. More than just the sex or her wealth. Nina wanted *her*.

"I believe you." Cassandra stroked Nina's hair and looked at her with a dreamy smile. Nina's heart fluttered. *I'm getting through to her!* She beamed with pride and devotion.

"We'll catch up tomorrow." Cassandra pulled away. "Enjoy everything I have to offer, meanwhile."

Nina's heart sank. "Tomorrow?!"

"I have other plans, my pet." Cassandra tucked Nina's hair behind her ear and held her gaze. "Don't be clingy, now."

Nina gulped. How could she not be clingy? She didn't come here to have Cassandra ignore her for the rest of the day! But even as she hated it, Nina knew better than to speak up. She lowered her shoulders and bowed her head. "I'm sorry, miss."

"Don't worry, pet," Cassandra dragged her thong up her gorgeous thighs. "You'll have plenty of time to worship me later."

The promise did nothing to soothe Nina. She threw herself on the bed the moment Cassandra left.

It took but a moment to get herself off, but she cried when she realized she would spend the night alone. Being so close to her dreams crushed Nina's heart, even as she scolded herself for making such a fuss. *You only just met her.* Nina groaned, rolling onto her side and scowling at herself. She repeated Cassandra's words. *Don't be clingy.* Nina's clashing emotions and the overwhelming nature of her arrangement made her lightheaded. She dozed off in her enormous, comfortable new bed, promising to explore Cassandra's mansion after a quick nap.

Exploration

CHAPTER 5

Nina stared at the garden and the lake from her balcony. The mansion was just miles away from civilization, but those miles were devoid of any other humans. Nina wondered if the Cardona family bought the land all around the lake. Maybe even the lake itself, if that were possible. She couldn't wait to tell Hope all about this place in person, but right now, Nina needed to get her bearings in her new life. The kitchen seemed as good a place to start as any, with her stomach growling.

Nina counted the time it took just to get from her room to the dining area—one minute and twelve seconds. She chuckled. *Nobody should live in such excess.* But Leslie, Miranda, and the other girls got to enjoy it as well. So many people to meet. It didn't seem as daunting anymore, not after Cassandra's approval. Their relationship was not normal, and it never would be, but Nina wasn't jealous of the other girls anymore—just curious.

Leslie greeted Nina as she entered the kitchen. She didn't hesitate to help with preparing lunch, following Leslie's lead as they made salads for a dozen people. Her time in college left Nina with little cooking skills, but Nina wanted to tackle the challenge and serve Cassandra with more than just sex. Making a good impression on the others came as a bonus.

"Can I ask you something?" Nina cut a few tomatoes into thick slices.

"Shoot," Leslie said.

"It's all going pretty fast," Nina said, focusing on not cutting herself. "I mean, not with Cassandra, but all of this. What are my duties going to be?"

"Don't worry about that. We have an app on our phones with all the chores. You just claim whatever you feel like doing."

Nina paused and frowned, looking for a sign of jest on her coworker's face.

"What?" Leslie stuffed her face with an egg while guiding Nina's work. "The job is more of a formality. We're not exactly drowning in work here."

"Wow." Nina had no more words to describe her surprise.

"I mean, we even convinced her to hire a company to do the cleaning. That was the only chore none of us enjoyed doing."

"Wait," Nina said, "we're here as her servants, but you got her to find others to do your work? How did you manage that?"

"She wants us here." Leslie winked. "We're just doing stuff we like so she can justify it to her mom. That mean old crow still controls the money, technically."

Nina shrugged. *So, even the billionaire has someone looking over her shoulder.*

Together, they whipped up a nice salad—with a little too much dressing—for the whole crew. Although she was no kitchen queen, Nina pictured herself helping every day. If that was good enough to stay here, she really was in heaven.

"So just to be clear," Nina put down two bowls on the huge wooden table, "how much work do you do on average? And what are the worst jobs?"

Leslie laughed as she handed over a few more plates and bowls. "You don't believe it, do you? I spend my days maintaining the cars and driving her around. For most of the girls, working four hours will be a busy day."

"No way," Nina said, still in disbelief. "And she pays you for this?"

"Three grand a month."

Nina nearly dropped the plates. *Three grand? To do some basic chores...and only the ones you like?* Nina pinched herself to make sure she wasn't dreaming.

Leslie tapped her phone as she said, "Crazy, right? What surprises me is that there are girls who come here, get the tour, then go 'Nah'."

Nina recalled the article Hope had shown her. That girl at least had an excuse, but who wouldn't sign up for this if all Cassandra required was friendship? She expressed her thoughts to her mentor.

Leslie waved her arms around. "Beats me. Cass has been nothing but awesome to us. Hell, I'd do the asslicking myself if she asked me, and I'm not even gay."

Leslie followed it up with a laugh. Nina's performance with Cassandra—and the brunette's incredible orgasm on her face—kept her from feeling jealous or threatened.

She wondered if there was a catch to all this, one she failed to see. Leslie sure seemed to enjoy her time as Cassandra's driver and fleet manager. There had to be a downside, but what? Nina didn't linger on these thoughts, smiling as another servant arrived.

"Aww, you must be Nina!" The thick redhead threw her arms around Nina in a tight, inappropriate hug—wearing a tight, inappropriate black dress. That kind of contact and outfit was normal around here, Nina reassured herself, embracing the servant as if they knew each other well. The redhead stood a little shorter than Nina, making her proportions even more exotic. *Cassandra knows how to pick them.*

"I'm Dora," she pulled away and smiled, "and everyone already made that joke, so don't."

"What, that you're adorable?" Nina said, empha-sizing Dora in 'adorable'.

Leslie laughed. "Smooth, Nina. Real smooth."

Dora shook her head and winked before taking a seat. Maybe Cassandra had that effect, but everyone seemed so at ease...even Nina herself. That flirta-tious reaction never would've left her lips before, not even when getting close to Hope.

A few more girls joined them. If it weren't all so incredibly amazing, the ordeal would've creeped her out. They were a flock of helpers that, apparently, worked and lived together like one big happy family. Nina half expected Cassandra to reveal herself as a vampire, or some cult leader.

But Cassandra didn't join them, so Nina spent the better part of an hour getting to know her new colleagues. She chatted with Tess, the equestrian, and Scarlett, a stylist. They welcomed Nina into her new home without judgment. Nina couldn't grasp that Cassandra didn't desire any of them, but she trusted her boss—and the servants—to be honest. Even if she just met them, they were all genuine, with stories just like hers. They were a bunch of failures, more or less, saved by a billionaire who didn't know how else to surround herself with friends. It seemed to work out, strange as it was.

NINA OFFERED TO HELP Dora and Leslie clean up, but they told her to find Jenny—the techie who managed all their electronics. Leslie gave directions to Jenny's lair, and Nina snorted. *You need directions to get around this place.* She timed that walk, too, but the three minutes didn't count—she got lost halfway through the maze. The gym seemed inviting, but she had to get her *gear*.

"Uh, hi?" Nina knocked on the open door of Jenny's dark room. The tech girl sat with her back to the door, her dyed blonde hair hanging messily down her shoulders. The tank top she wore stood out from the designer dresses favored by the others.

"Nina," Jenny turned and beckoned her to enter, "Cassandra's latest catch. Do you like it?"

The question wasn't very specific, but the answer was yes, regardless. Nina liked it all. The mansion, the clothes, and the job. Jenny's room was impressive as well, if the tech girl hinted at that, with a dozen monitors and large computers. Nina didn't doubt that Cassandra bought whatever the nerdy girl required with no regard for the expenses.

One of the larger screens showed a view of the area from above. Nina leaned in to look at it. "Wow…she's got her own satellite?"

"Drones, dummy," Jenny said with a smile. "Fully automated, but I can control them if I want."

She demonstrated it with the joysticks on her desk. If she told Nina they stood in a NASA control center, she would believe it. Maps with colored dots, flashing labels, and various pop-ups cluttered the monitors.

"*She* is going to space, though." Jenny rummaged through a pile of electronics. She mentioned the planned adventure like it was a trip to the coffee shop.

"Space?" Nina asked, dumbfounded. She pointed up. "As in...?"

"Oh yes. Space. The final frontier." Jenny chucked a phone Nina's way. She frowned when Nina did. "Star Trek? No?"

Nina shook my head. "Sorry. Is she going alone?"

"Yeah. That shit's expensive, even for her."

Jenny took her job—or hobby—seriously, requiring the newcomer to pick a twelve-digit code for the phone before allowing Nina to toy with it. The large, foldable device contained apps for just about everything around the modern palace. It took Jenny over two hours to explain it all, and Nina's constant questions didn't speed things up, either.

"IT'S A LOT TO TAKE IN," Nina said, trying to memorize all the options. Car keys, alarm systems, credit cards—Jenny made sure the girls had access to everything they needed.

"My number is in there, if you're ever lost," Jenny said. "And if you hold the button on the side, the private security swoops in to escort you out of danger."

Nina gulped. "Is that necessary?"

Jenny swiveled on her chair and cocked her head. "You're a way into Cassandra's multi-billion dollar life. Trust me, you'll feel better knowing these guys are around."

Nina had not considered that. She didn't regret her decisions, but she had seen enough movies of abductions involving rich people—or their loved ones. Being monitored and followed didn't bother her as much as the fact it might very well be necessary. *Perhaps that's the red flag?*

"Hey, it's not that bad," Jenny said. "We've made everything as secure as possible, and we rarely have an incident."

Jenny's confidence put Nina only a little at ease, even if she wanted to believe it. "I guess..."

"How about this. Give the emergency call a try when you're outside. You'll see for yourself."

"I can do that?" Nina asked.

"I have them run drills all the time. They get paid top dollar to keep us safe. Besides, they love showing their skills. Bunch of cowboys."

Those plans soothed Nina somewhat. She figured Cassandra had hired the best of security. Nina smirked at the idea of a bunch of black SUVs screeching to a stop and big, burly men clearing a path for her. That was male attention she did approve of.

"Well, I think you're all set," Jenny said. "Hey, with Cassandra out for the rest of the day, what do you plan on doing?"

The question blanked Nina's mind. She hadn't really thought about the possibilities and freedom. The huge gym appealed, but so did going for a swim—in the pool or the lake. Or she could go relax in the library or cinema. Yet, for all the ways she could keep herself busy, Nina mostly wanted to get to know Cassandra better.

"Ah, I get it." Jenny giggled. "There's not much to do around here, right?"

Nina snorted. "Yeah, that's it. It's just so overwhelming."

"Believe it or not, you actually get used to it."

"I'll take your word for it," Nina said. "I think I'll introduce herself to the rest."

Jenny nodded and sat back down. "Remember, you can check everyone's schedule in the calendar app. Have fun!"

NINA HAD WALKED FOR HOURS in and around the mansion by the time she met everyone. Every servant was welcoming and kind, and her calendar for the next weeks filled up rapidly. Just when she thought she memorized the maze, Nina somehow ended up in the gym again. Nina texted Jenny, thanking the techie for the life-saving calendar and maps on her new phone. It seemed impossible to keep track of everything manually. She made her way back to the lounge, crashing on a couch so soft she sunk a few inches into the thick fabric. Her legs thanked her for the respite, burning from all the rushing around. She pulled up the aptly named work app to find out what chores were available.

To Jenny's credit, the system she created had everything laid out. Every type of job or errand had check marks, color coding, and rankings for varying levels of urgency and preference. Nina chuckled as she scrolled through the long list for the upcoming days, finding just about all the jobs already claimed by the others. A fair amount of it had orange labels, meaning the girls didn't mind someone else taking over or helping. Nina added her name to a few jobs —cooking and tending to the horses. Dora had signed up to make breakfast, but Nina put down a green check mark to show she wanted to help. Or rather, to learn.

It left Nina with plenty of free time, just as Leslie had implied. She texted Leslie to ask if any of the cars were available for personal use. It would be nice to pick up Hope in something more luxurious than the old rust bucket.

"All of them, dear," Leslie responded. "Just check the car app to reserve a time slot."

"Including the egg?" Nina typed back before switching to the app and confirming it herself. *Including the Koenigsegg.*

"Don't worry about Cass if you scratch it," Leslie replied. "Worry about me. I'll kill you and they'll never find your body."

Cute emojis followed the threats, but she made her point clear. Perhaps the absurd, mysterious car wasn't the best choice. But the idea of showing off something so rare put an arrogant grin on Nina's face. *If you've got it...*

Nina reserved the car and planned a much-needed chat with Hope, who wanted to know all the dirty details.

The absurdity of it all finally dawned on her, and she laughed out loud with nobody around to hear it. With everything slowly falling into place, Nina enjoyed the pleasures of her new home. After an invigorating workout and a long swim, Leslie and Jenny invited her for dinner and a movie—which became a marathon of Star Trek films at Jenny's insistence.

With her promise to help Dora with breakfast at seven in the morning, Nina reluctantly declined to stick around for yet another movie. They had plenty of time to hang out later. Jenny playfully held on to Nina's hand until she pinky-promised to watch *all* Star Trek shows together over the next few months.

Nina dragged herself back to her bedroom, her head spinning. The leisure time with her new friends had somehow relaxed her a little, but the exhausting first day of her new life had drained her. She threw herself on her bed, snoring within seconds of closing her eyes. Leslie's words drove her to pleasant dreams. *You'll eat her out when she has breakfast.*

Breakfast

CHAPTER 6

Nina didn't dare open her eyes, afraid she was back in her dorm room—and that everything had just been a crazy dream. But the mattress was way too soft for that. Birds chirped on her balcony. Nina opened her eyes and peeked through the window. A row of tiny, fluffy finches sang their morning song for her, hopping about with as much care as the women Nina met yesterday. Nina rubbed her eyes with a yawn. The birds woke her mere minutes before the alarm would have. She had slept without interruption, but the overwhelming introduction to Cassandra's world left her completely spent.

With about an hour to prepare, Nina forced herself out of bed and into the bathroom. With a dozen creams and lotions, she had everything she needed to get ready for the day. Scarlett, Nina's new stylist, would have her head for it, but Nina didn't put on that much makeup—just enough to make her face shine the way her heart did. Cassandra chose Nina for who she was, after all. She planned to save the heavy makeup for special occasions, of which there would surely be many.

Clothing was another matter, however. Although she had a knack for scoring affordable outfits, Nina twirled like a princess in the changing room, unable to choose between the countless gorgeous dresses. *Dior. Bottega Veneta.* Her fingers touched thousand-dollar fabrics. Within a minute, Nina had picked out half a dozen options before her eyes settled on an absurd maid outfit. The black satin minidress wasn't a professional uniform, nor did it seem as well-made as the luxury brands. But dressing up as a maid for her master made her grin wickedly. She held it in front of her bare body. The bottom was too short to be anything but a playful attire, and the frilly accents were ridiculous. *It's perfect!*

After putting it all on, Nina snickered at how silly she looked in the disgraceful costume. No real maid would wear this, which helped sell her devotion to Cassandra. Nina put on a pair of impractical stilettos to complete the attire and went to the kitchen to earn her place in Cassandra's life.

Dora laughed when she saw Nina, but the redhead beckoned her into a friendly hug.

"You don't play around, do you?" Dora adjusted the ruffled headband of the maid.

Nina smiled and gave a little curtsy. "Ready to work!"

"Good, I always welcome the help. Come on, let's make some strawberry pancakes."

Dora gave a quick course on baking pancakes. With the sizeable amount of people to serve, Nina had ample opportunity to learn.

"Go on, have some. I've got this." Dora nudged Nina at the stack of pancakes they just made. With the sweet aroma and her growling belly, Nina didn't need to be told twice. She put some extra syrup on the warm pancakes and gorged down on her creations.

"Oof, not bad," Nina said with her mouth full. "This is worth waking up early for!"

Dora winked as she slid another pancake onto a plate while filling the pan at the same time. Her talent impressed Nina, who smiled in admiration. Nina never planned on a culinary career, but it became an appealing prospect in her new home. She pictured herself doing this every day with pleasure.

"So, how long have you been here?" Nina joined Dora once more after finishing her third pancake.

"Two years now," Dora said. "After getting discharged from the Army."

"No way?" Nina stopped to rub the woman's shoulder. "I'm sorry."

"I'm not. It's the best thing that ever happened to me. Look at where it got me!"

Nina entertained that line of thought. Whatever their past, the girls all ended up in Cassandra and her unexpected, generous lifestyle. Whether they got there through fate or dumb luck, Nina reasoned it was better to enjoy the result than wallow in their history. She didn't ask about the discharge...even if she was curious.

Leslie joined them after about half an hour. She needed a moment to catch her breath after laughing hysterically at Nina's outfit.

"Oh, Nina," Leslie sniffled, "you look so stupid in that. I love it."

"Yeah, yeah." Nina handed her a plate, her cheeks flushed. "I just want to show her how much I appreciate being here."

Nina's heart skipped a beat upon hearing Cassandra's voice. "I'm glad you feel that way."

It was the third time the billionaire got the drop on Nina. *Maybe she is a vampire.* Nina yanked the plate out of Leslie's hands and spun around. "Ah! Good morning, miss!"

The corners of Cassandra's lips curled up, turning her resting bitch face into a doting smile. She bowed her head slightly as she took the pancakes. "Thank you, dear."

Cassandra's gratitude warmed Nina's heart. As much as she loved the billionaire's brattiness, approval still felt better. Cassandra strutted away in her white gown, her ass barely hidden under the sheer fabric. *No panties.*

"Time to work," Leslie whispered in Nina's ear. Leslie had already taken another plate, appearing indifferent to how rudely Nina had snatched the previous one. Nina glanced at her fellow blonde with a frown.

"Morning routine, remember?" Leslie stroked Nina's chin with her thumb. "You eat her out when she eats…"

Nina gulped. Cassandra sat down at the wide, long table, her gown split open between her firm breasts. *Now? With everyone in the room?* Nina's expression conveyed her confusion.

"Go on, now." Leslie slapped Nina's ass. "Before she finishes her meal."

Nina's heart fluttered at the command. As relaxed as Leslie and Dora were around her, going down on Cassandra while they watched wasn't something Nina expected. But their encouraging smiles—and her love for Cassandra—carried her over any doubts.

Nina walked over to Cassandra, who hadn't yet commented on the maid's outfit. She looked up and cocked her head, faking indifference. It was too late for her to hide the pleasure she took in Nina's submission, but Nina played along for her master's amusement.

"Can I be of further assistance, miss?" Nina bowed down beside Cassandra, holding her hands in front of the tiny apron around her waist. She recalled how she thought about a similar encounter just yesterday in the coffee shop. Now she got to play the role she dreamed of.

"You know what to do, pet." Cassandra narrowed her eyes and spread her legs—just enough to reinforce her point. She looked away, pretending to ignore Nina.

"Of course, miss!" Nina crawled under the table and settled between Cassandra's legs. Cassandra's arousal quickly replaced the sweet scent of Nina's pancakes. For all her high-and-mighty attitude, Cassandra's body language betrayed her. Her legs jerked when Nina's fingers touched her thighs, and she moaned when soft lips followed.

Nina's confidence grew with each opportunity to please Cassandra, whose eagerness made her easy to satisfy. Soon she wouldn't know a world without Nina. Where college failed to excite her, Cassandra provided Nina with determination and goals. She ignored Cassandra's pussy, tending to her lover's warm thighs instead. Cassandra was so sensitive Nina almost believed she could get her lover off this way. She nibbled the thick thighs ever so slightly, and Cassandra rewarded her by squeezing her head between them. Cassandra's natural aroma hung heavier here, taking Nina back to yesterday's submission.

The lure of Cassandra's treasure clashed with that of her own. Nina allowed herself to move her hands under her satin skirt. Nina wore no panties either, giving her easy access to her needy pussy. The table kept her from enjoying Cassandra's gorgeous face, but it also gave her the freedom to play with herself—without risking a scolding. Nina teased her labia while peppering Cassandra's inner thighs with affection, slipping a finger into her pussy before tending to her lover. Cassandra let Nina play the long game, her voice remaining quiet as she had her breakfast.

Just as Nina got into a rhythm with her fingers, chairs sliding behind her startled her so much that she bumped her head against the table. Cassandra's thighs clasped around Nina's head when she tried to back away. The surrounding voices confirmed her curiosity.

"Good morning, boss," Jenny said. "Isn't it?"

Her question lacked any subtlety. Nina blushed at how awkward the whole scenario was. She watched a few movies with the nerdy girl less than twelve hours ago, and now Jenny sat down at a table, knowing full well Nina licked Cassandra's pussy.

"It could be better, Jenny." Cassandra tightened her legs. "It's a slow start…"

Nina wondered if the comment included a command. The risk of disappointment weighed heavier than the joy of teasing, so Nina took the hint and shuffled forward. Another girl sat down somewhere behind her, but she ignored it. With their faces out of sight, their existence didn't matter…as much.

Jenny talked with someone—Tess, judging by the Texan accent—as if Nina wasn't even there. Two others took a seat, their conversations turning into a mix of activity while Nina tended to the one woman who remained silent.

Cassandra's excitement grew when Nina kissed her lips. She twitched and whimpered, barely noticeable but clear enough for the maid. Cassandra's toned belly and the underside of her breasts were as far as Nina could look, but the flower in front of her was all she needed to see. Cassandra relaxed a little —until Nina kissed again.

When Nina's tongue wiggled between Cassandra's labia, giggles from the other servants joined Cassandra's soft coos. It stirred the butterflies in Nina's stomach. She gave her lover more, hoping to draw out louder reactions. Cassandra's angelic voice influenced Nina as well—every whimper sent a surge of heat down her body. Nina withdrew from Cassandra's pussy, and her own, to focus on their clits.

Cassandra bucked wildly when Nina's lips brushed her button. The girls were equally sensitive. Recent events left Nina high on lust, and the best way to ride it out was by making her lover come. Strong thighs hugged Nina's face when she licked Cassandra's clit. She mimicked the shaky movements on her hand as she rubbed her own pussy. More than the act itself, Nina became lightheaded from the casual conversations of Cassandra's staff.

"Boss, what do you think?" Jenny asked. The others stopped talking, leaving only Nina's squelching kisses and Cassandra's cries.

"Well, ah, if you think it'll work." Cassandra sang her words as she humped her servant's face. Nina gave her no break, especially now. Without her usual, annoyingly perfect tone, Cassandra said, "I trust you'll...fuck...make the right decision."

The surrender in Cassandra's voice filled Nina with pride. She lowered to kiss her lover's pussy, smooching firmly to draw out more giggles while finding the right pressure on Cassandra's clit.

"Oh, come on!" Leslie slammed the table. "She can't be *that* good."

Nina almost broke away to laugh, but Cassandra's ever-increasing wetness captivated her. The way Leslie spoke about her made Nina's pussy spasm, and she rubbed her clit even harder.

"Yeah, Linda barely got you to blush," Scarlett chimed in. "But Nina's a lot sluttier, isn't she?"

Cassandra held on tight, perhaps expecting Nina's reaction. She wanted to deny Scarlett's claim, but how could she? While it wasn't the life she expected, Nina didn't hesitate to throw herself at the feet of the beautiful billionaire. Scarlett's remark drove Nina to tend to Cassandra—and herself—even more. *Yes, I am a slut, and that's all right!*

"She's eager, at least." Dora kicked Nina's butt. "I can smell her. Or is that you, Cass?"

Cassandra's moans filled the room, while her pussy muffled Nina's whimpers. The girls laughed, making Nina's head spin. It became harder to focus on Cassandra, but she fought the dizziness.

"Probably both," Leslie said. "I'm pretty sure Nina gets off on it. Dirty slut."

Whether it was the eager tongue or Leslie's words that did it, Cassandra clamped down on Nina and whimpered. She held her lover between her thick thighs, and Nina recognized the high from the quivering of Cassandra's vagina. Diving in just a little deeper, she French kissed her dear lover while pinching and slapping her own clit. But even as Cassandra drenched her face and sang her name, Nina's climax eluded her.

"Oh, god." Cassandra slammed against her maid. "Nina...!"

Her admiration drove her staff to laughter. Nina closed her eyes and lapped Cassandra's pussy, drinking her juices with gulps she hoped her lover could hear. Cassandra's vagina massaged Nina's tongue as she wiggled inside, keeping the wave of ecstasy going for a little while longer.

Even when the muscles of Cassandra's legs and pussy relaxed, Nina kept kissing and licking, drunk on the taste and chasing her high.

"She's still going?" Jenny asked. Nina's pulse raced when one of the heavy chairs moved over the floor.

"Oh my fucking god," Jenny said, her voice now much closer. "She really is a slut."

The brazen comment of Jenny, and her peeking under the table, gave Nina that last nudge. She withdrew her tongue and moaned loud enough for everyone to hear. Kneeling in a maid's outfit, bringing Cassandra to orgasm, and Jenny's chirpy remarks—it all came together in Nina's lust-addled mind. She trembled on the floor, her feet kicking against the hardwood while clenching her thighs around her wrist. She pressed down on her clit hard, punishing herself playfully. Her whole body tensed up. She leaned against Cassandra's pussy, whimpering while kissing her lover's lips. The giggles of her coworkers drew out Nina's thrill, and Cassandra's fingers coming down to run through her hair kept her shuddering and moaning.

"I think she's coming," Jenny said, still snooping under the table. "Or she's having a seizure."

"Jenny!" Dora said. "Don't be an asshole."

Nina rested against Cassandra's thigh as she came down from her high. With all that happened, she didn't dare come up from her hiding spot. She kissed and licked Cassandra some more, waiting for everyone to leave. But they didn't get up. Only Jenny moved, getting back in her seat.

"Think she's gonna stay there all morning?" Jenny asked, taunting Nina.

"I can hear you!" Nina blurted out, hoping they'd get the point. But her weak voice only made the women giggle more.

Even though she didn't regret any of it, a pang of shame pricked Nina's heart. Her new friends supported her, but she couldn't blame anyone for teasing her. When Nina crawled away from her submissive position and got back up, Leslie and the others cheered. Nina almost sank through her wobbly knees with a reddened face. But Cassandra took her hand and smiled—and everything else washed away.

Riding Lessons

CHAPTER 7

Nina's head still spun after the breakfast encounter. She had barely noticed the looks on
everyone's faces, but the way Cassandra held her
hand made a world of difference. Nina wanted more
of that, a lot more. She wanted to become Cassandra's girlfriend—not just her lover or a sex toy. She
scoffed at her thoughts as she retreated to her bedroom. *Cassandra is an entitled, bratty billionaire.
She'll never love you. Not really.*

And yet, as hard as she tried to convince herself,
it just didn't take. Instead, another voice nagged at
her. *Why not?* Cassandra lived in a different world.
One where trust and friendship were scarce. Nina
stared at herself in the mirror. *I'll get to her heart.
No matter what it takes.*

One obstacle impeded her plans. With Cassandra
at home, Nina didn't feel like doing any chores—or
even any leisure. Even if she could fill her day with
different activities every five minutes, all she wanted
to do was spend more time with Cassandra.

However, she had promised Tess to work at the ranch, so that's what she set out to do. *Earn your place, Nina.*

"HOWDY!" TESS TIPPED HER COWBOY HAT as she commanded her horse to a stop. Nina grinned, more so at how stereotypical Tess appeared than at her loud greeting. The thick accent reminded Nina of one of her high school teachers, who prided herself as a born-and-raised Texan. Nina often pictured the middle-aged woman in her younger years. Tess fit those imaginations to a T, wearing boots with spurs, a flannel shirt with a sleeveless denim jacket, and a cowboy hat.

"Hey, Tess. I feel silly in my outfit now," Nina leaned on the fence. She picked out what she assumed was a proper rider's fit, with figure-hugging, stretchy pants and a cute polo. The cap on her head made her feel anything but sexy.

"Nonsense. You're a looker." Tess dismounted the horse with elegance and came up to the fence. "It got nothing on the maid's outfit, though."

Nina blushed and walked alongside Tess to the gate. "Change of subject."

"Too late to be shy about it, girl."

Nina opened the gate for Tess, patting the horse that followed. "Word of warning. I know nothing about horses."

"That's all right. With the way you handle Cassandra, Rob here ought to be a cakewalk."

"I'm not sure I can handle Cassandra," Nina took the reins Tess handed her. "And what kind of name is Rob for a horse, anyway?"

Tess guided Nina and Rob to the stables, where she fastened the reins around a pole. "Short for Robinson. Cassandra likes to name them horses after investigators that bother her. Y'know, FBI, IRS, and so on."

Although the stench of these animals filled the air, Nina didn't mind. She took a moment to show affection to each horse while Tess grabbed another saddle and reins.

"Uh, what's that for?" Nina asked. She opened the chest-high door of Kenny—one of the other horses. Nina shook her head as she thought about how some poor sucker got a horse named after him. These investigations might have been legitimate, but that didn't spook her much. She didn't approve of the rich getting richer, yet she also didn't believe most people with wealth were criminals by nature. Certainly not Cassandra.

"This is for you." Tess gently placed the saddle on the horse's back and tossed Nina the reins. "Put that over yonder. Come here and see how it's done."

Nina put her hand on Kenny's side while observing Tess' technique. "I thought I came here to brush them or something."

"We've got stable hands for that. You can learn how to train them with me, but if you just want to ride them, that's cool. These animals need plenty of love, too, you hear?" Tess showed how to fit the various straps for Kenny's comfort, then undid it all so Nina could try. It took a few tries before Tess approved of it.

"I'm still not sure what Cassandra needs from me, exactly," Nina said as Tess guided her to put on the bridle. "But if it's possible, I'd love to help you out here."

"That's the spirit!" Tess slapped Nina's shoulders with the strength of, well, a horse. "And don't you worry none. You already figured out exactly what Cassandra wants from you."

Nina lowered her head in shame when Tess held her ring and index finger in the shape of a V and stuck out her tongue. She rubbed Nina's shoulder before hugging her, while Kenny neighed and bumped his head against the girls. Awkward as everything was, there was nowhere Nina would rather be.

She followed Tess' instructions and redid the whole getup for the horse, repeating it until she got it right without thinking. Nina feared she'd forget it before the end of the day but, just like the cooking, she'd get the hang of it, eventually.

With her teacher's guidance, Nina walked Kenny outside and learned how to tie a proper knot. Her attention wavered when she saw someone approach her. Someone wearing an outfit just like hers, rather than a cowgirl fit like Tess. Someone she had finally managed not to think about for a few minutes.

"Pet." Cassandra winked at Nina before turning to face Tess. "Good morning. All ready?"

"All set, boss," Tess said. "Have fun, y'all."

Nina stared in shock as Tess walked off, leaving the reins in her hand.

"Hold up," Nina stammered, but Cassandra already took Rob's reins.

"Come on, pet." Cassandra got up in the stirrup and swung her leg over the horse's back, landing softly in the saddle. "Just follow my lead."

Nina surprised herself with the ease with which she got into the saddle. *Not bad.* She copied Cassandra as best she could. The way she held the reins.

How her back arched, making her even sexier. Cassandra clicked her tongue, trotting off into the open. Fields she owned, like so much else. Nina used to think about what it'd be like to be a millionaire sometimes—now she chased after a billionaire who spent money in ways Nina couldn't even fathom.

RIDING THROUGH THE FIELDS around the lake calmed Nina's lustful heart, even with her beautiful boss bouncing up and down beside her. It gave her a glimpse of a more relaxed side of Cassandra. Nina smiled at how unusual things were in their relationship. While she had no doubts about their sexual future, the uncertainty of the friendship and romance went shook her core.

"Not that bad, is it?" Cassandra stroked her horse's neck while slowing down. Kenny required a little more tugging and mumbling from Nina to come to a stop.

"I wasn't sure what to expect." Nina gazed at the outrageous mansion from across the lake. Cassandra owned everything within a ten-mile radius. Sitting on a horse in a peaceful field, with not much of a job expected of her, Nina couldn't believe her luck. She stared at her new home as she scratched her horse's head.

"Me neither," Cassandra said. Her horse walked around a bit as the women talked. "I'm glad you're okay with this arrangement."

"Of course I am. But I'm here for you if you want…more."

Nina's heart sank when Cassandra looked away and, after a brief pause, clicked her tongue to make her horse trot on. Nina closed her eyes and sighed. *Great. You blew it, idiot.* She cursed herself as she followed. She also cursed Cassandra for avoiding the matter. Was it that hard to talk about exploring more than just sex?

Neither of the women spoke, and Nina's gut wrenched with every passing minute. After tasting this new life of luxury, she already dreaded losing it. Still, she couldn't stand the uncertainty of her relationship with Cassandra. Her heart grew heavy. She almost reached the point of calling her lover out.

Cassandra halted her horse suddenly, and Nina scrambled to stop Kenny as well.

"Everyone's out for my money," Cassandra said. She sighed and glared at Nina. "I just want us to be clear about what we have. Please?"

Nina trembled with anxiety. Her aching heart made her speak out. "No. I'm sorry, Cassandra. You're wrong."

"Excuse me?" Cassandra nudged her horse closer and scowled at Nina.

"I can't imagine what it's like, to be so rich and afraid to trust people. But you came looking for me, okay? I didn't even know you."

Cassandra exhaled sharply, the stressful sound rising over the horses' whinnying.

"I know it's weird, all of this." Nina's voice cracked as she feared ruining her chances. "But I'm not after your possessions. I…I'm here for you."

She closed her eyes and waited for Cassandra to lash out, ride off, or otherwise make clear she didn't trust it. The uneasy wiggling of Kenny made Nina shuffle in her saddle. If these animals sensed emotion, Kenny couldn't be unluckier.

"Why?" Cassandra asked after an eerie silence. She leaned in and grabbed Nina's chin. "What's there to like about me?"

Nina lowered her shoulders. "Cass..."

"No, tell me. I heard what your friend said. How I'm your type because I'm a bratty billionaire. Right? We just met. So, tell me. Why do you like me?"

"I don't know!" Nina pulled away. "Okay? I don't know what I like about you. I just do."

She got off the horse, feeling trapped in the saddle and stirrups. She stared at the forest in the distance. As Cassandra dismounted her horse as well, Nina took a few steps away from her.

"Everybody hates me." Cassandra closed in to put her hand on Nina's shoulder. "It's why I'm paying you not to care."

"That's pathetic." Nina jerked away. "Money isn't your problem. It's..."

Cassandra forced Nina to make eye contact. "Then what?"

"Actually," Nina narrowed her eyes, "I don't believe you. If you just wanted sex, you have a dozen girls who would gladly be an emotionless sex doll for you."

Cassandra frowned, but Nina wasn't done. "I'm not gonna lie. I absolutely want to live like this. But I can't do it if you won't talk to me."

Nina rambled on. "No, I don't want to hear it. I'm not saying you should love me already. But you can't jerk me around and treat me like a toy. I have feelings, you know!"

Nina took a deep breath, preparing to unleash more. Cassandra shushed her with a finger.

"So do I," she whispered. "I just can't afford to be vulnerable."

Nina pouted. "Can't or won't?"

Cassandra stared into Nina's eyes for a while. "I can't promise you anything."

"I'm not asking you to. I just want a fucking chance!"

Cassandra's chuckle broke Nina's love-stoked fury enough to bring her down a few notches.

"What?" Nina asked.

"Nothing." Cassandra's smile broadened as she glanced away. "You're different from the others, that's all."

Nina scoffed. "You're damn right, I am."

Cassandra laughed, and said, "Be careful, pet, or I'll have to punish you for your arrogance."

"Try it." Nina crossed her arms. She yelped when Cassandra grabbed her hair and tugged on it.

"Oh, I will." Cassandra drove Nina to her hands and knees, then sat her full weight down on her back. Nina groaned. She struggled to stay upright, muttering about how her hands and expensive pants got all dirty. It was just an excuse to ignore her true feelings. With just that simple act, Cassandra reawakened Nina's submissive lust again. Though her pulse still raced with the unsatisfying outburst of her romantic needs, she couldn't deny the erotic effect of Cassandra perched on her back with both feet at her sides.

"Even my horses are better trained than you," Cassandra said. She tightened her thighs against Nina's sides, clicking her tongue as she slapped Nina's ass. "Giddy-up!"

Nina strained under Cassandra's pressure and the stinging of her ass, yet she remained in place. "What are you, twelve?"

Cassandra tugged on Nina's hair, which she had aptly fitted into a ponytail.

"Don't pretend you don't like this." Cassandra moved her hand to rub Nina's pussy through her pants. The effect was immediate. Nina scolded herself for spreading her legs a little. She lowered her head, but Cassandra yanked it back up.

"Come on, pretty pony." Cassandra bounced on Nina's back. "Tell me you like it."

Nina struggled not to admit it, especially when Cassandra's fingers played with her pussy through her clothes. While the layered fabrics of her pants and thong made the stimulation far too subdued, Nina enjoyed the mistreatment. It buried the rush of her emotional outburst under one of pure lust.

"If you admit it, I'll spank you." Cassandra squeezed Nina's ass.

"That's not much of a—"

The loud slap made Nina moan like a slut. They both knew the truth. Spanking Nina most certainly was a reward, and she couldn't deny it any more than her deeper feelings for Cassandra. She swallowed her pride—just the way she loved it.

"I like it, miss," Nina hissed through her clenched teeth. She knew it lacked conviction. Cassandra gave a playful thwack on her butt, regardless.

"What was that?" Cassandra teased Nina's ass and pussy with her fingers.

"I like it when you ride me," Nina said, drowning out her heartache with her submissive side. The immediate rewards made her jiggle under her rider. She let it all out. With no one around to judge her for it, Nina begged Cassandra for more while she shook her ass, enticing her lover. Cassandra kept holding on to Nina's hair, but she stopped spanking to focus on roughly rubbing Nina's pussy instead. "Are you my pretty pet?"

Nina bit her lip and arched her back, almost throwing her lover off. It wasn't the teasing of her pussy that got her off. The absurdity of her submission, out in a muddy field somewhere, drove Nina crazy. Even after just admitting her desires, Nina got treated like a pet, and her self-loathing fueled the fires in her core. Her legs trembled. She fought the urge to just plop down into the grass while Cassandra slapped and fingered her cunt. Nina's continuous moans startled the horses as she sang out her lover's name in pure bliss. Cassandra played her part, cupping Nina's sex through the pants and tightening her legs around Nina's waist.

Nina's extensive wardrobe proved more than a luxury—whenever she had her fun with Cassandra, Nina drenched her panties.

NINA'S MUSCLES BURNED by the time Cassandra got up, though she didn't move until she got permission. Giggling, she rose to her feet and tried to clean her hands on her beige pants. She smiled wryly at Cassandra. "I'm sorry for dumping all that on you."

"It's okay." Cassandra stroked Nina's hair and tidied it up as much as possible. "But please accept that this is what I need from you…for now."

Although it hurt Nina that Cassandra couldn't open up to her, she calmed down enough to realize relationships worked both ways. It wasn't fair to demand anything of Cassandra, not so soon into their wicked relationship. Nina exhaled and nodded. "For now."

While Cassandra shook her head, she didn't shut Nina down. She held out her hand. Nina took it without hesitation.

"Good thing they didn't wander off too far," Nina said. She carefully approached Kenny while Cassandra lured Rob with kissing sounds. Nina smiled when they both got back in the saddle. It crushed her heart that her declaration of love went unanswered, but she didn't lose hope. *I will win her love!*

Nina spent the rest of the day without Cassandra, which hurt more than her emotional outburst and the way Cassandra shut her down. Even when she went swimming, or while playing tennis with Leslie, Nina kept replaying the conversation in her head. Her own words stuck out the most. *I don't know why I like you. I just do.*

Curling Egg

CHAPTER 8

Nina prepared herself for the same ritual. Maid outfit. Breakfast. Crawling under the table. To her welcome surprise, Dora and the others were all done before Cassandra arrived, giving Nina a more relaxed—yet still awkward—time alone with her lover.

Nina struggled to perform her best. Her stomach churned with unanswered feelings, and Cassandra didn't respond as much to her submission under the table, either.

By the time they were done, Nina crawled away, ready to bail out of there with uncertainty filling her mind. But Cassandra took her hand, gently caressing it.

"I have a meeting in a bit," Cassandra said. "Come along. I think you'll understand my position a little better when you meet them."

"Cassandra, I understand you just fine," Nina said. She clenched her teeth when she heard herself —she sounded way too judgmental. "I'm sorry. I didn't mean it like that."

Cassandra smiled wryly. "No, it's okay. But you don't understand my world. I'll have to show you."

Nina bit her lip. "It sounds a lot sexier when you put it like that."

"Oh, trust me, those meetings are the exact opposite of sexy." Cassandra stroked Nina's cheek. "But let's make sure you're irresistible either way."

Nina had no objections to that under any circumstance. The knot in her stomach faded as Cassandra hugged her close on the way to Nina's bedroom. While she still had to learn how to deal with Cassandra's reluctance for more, Nina reminded herself that any moment with Cassandra was a blessing.

CASSANDRA HANDED NINA A ONE-PIECE swimsuit she picked from the wardrobe. "Put that on, dear."

Nina swayed her hips as she strutted over to the small bench, putting on a show. She turned around and smiled seductively, not one bit shy of her naked body. Cassandra didn't mask the appreciation in her eyes. The rush that had filled Nina's core the moment she met Cassandra showed no signs of waning. She rode the high with newfound confidence. *Whatever happens, don't give up on her.* She bent forward as she lowered to put on the lovely swimwear, dragging it up slowly around her hips.

Focusing on Cassandra's deep brown eyes, Nina tried to pinpoint what the billionaire desired the most. Though Nina's hips weren't as wide as Dora's, her best friend always commended the long, toned legs. Cassandra seemed to enjoy them, too, but her eyes went all over Nina's body. Nina trailed her sides as she pulled the swimsuit over her belly, pressing her breasts together before covering them up. Everyone in the mansion had bigger tits, but Cassandra still couldn't keep her eyes off Nina's breasts when she bounced playfully.

"How do I look?" Nina twirled on her feet. She ran her hands over the smooth fabric, loving the expensive outfit. The dark blue swimsuit wrapped her figure perfectly. She made a note to thank Miranda for it when she got the chance. Most of her regular swimwear lacked a tight fit, but this tailored piece sat snug around her belly, breasts, and hips. The thong-like bottom snaked between her ass cheeks. She turned to present them to her wealthy lover.

Cassandra put her warm hands on Nina's bare butt, squeezing the soft cheeks possessively. "You're perfect."

Nina smiled in the mirror, her mind a little hazy at the sight of the tall billionaire groping her from behind. The attention and approval washed away any doubts she had. *Just be patient.* As much as Cassandra avoided the meat of the matter, she couldn't keep her hands off Nina.

"Pick out some sexy heels and jewelry." Cassandra kissed Nina's neck. "Then meet me downstairs in a few minutes."

Whimpering as Cassandra's hands—and breath—disappeared, leaving her eager for more, Nina nodded. "Yes, miss."

Cassandra's joyful laugh sent a rush down to her pussy. Cassandra gave a quick peck on Nina's cheek. "You really are eager."

Nina beamed, finding no shame in admitting it. As Cassandra left her to complete her outfit, Nina looked around the wardrobe with a satisfying sigh. There was so much to choose from. She jumped a little when she realized she could wear something new every day for at least half a year. By then, Miranda would no doubt come around with new collections.

For now, Nina kept herself from checking out all the dresses. She browsed the dozens of stiletto heels, ignoring the various pumps, sandals, and boots— even if she couldn't wait to try them all on. *Don't keep Cass waiting.*

One pair of heels matched the swimsuit perfectly, with gems on the straps similar to those on the one-piece. Nina put them on quickly, recalling Cassandra's timeframe, but she couldn't resist another peek at her mirror image. The gems on her dark swimsuit formed a diamond over her belly, showing off her navel and a few inches around it. She would never buy something like that—price notwithstanding— because she thought it more daring than a low-cut cleavage or skimpy bikini. With this design, the wearer displayed pride in her tight tummy. Nina was glad she spent enough time in the gym to make it work, trailing her fingers over her abs. Around the rear, sparkling gems decorated the swimwear, with most of her skin exposed. The perfectly tailored piece left no gaps between the fabric and her skin, making it her favorite swimwear she had ever worn by far.

Nina forced herself away from the mirror to pick out some jewelry. She gasped when she opened a drawer. The glistening necklaces, armbands, and rings looked like they could belong to royalty. The only accessories she ever wore were a simple necklace that belonged to her grandma or the braided, colorful armband Hope bought off a street vendor in

Paris. *Oh, Hope. I can't wait to show you all of this!*

While it seemed weird to wear any jewelry with a swimsuit, Nina didn't plan on wasting the chance to enjoy all this beauty. Following Cassandra's preference, she picked out small button earrings and a thin bracelet—shiny silver to fit her style. For a necklace, Nina settled on a simple chain with a tiny heart dangling from it. She took another last peek in the mirror, grinning at herself. *I can get used to this!*

She finished the outfit with a Birkin handbag—worth more than the college tuition she blew—before hurrying down the maze of the mansion to meet up with Cassandra.

CASSANDRA ALREADY WAITED FOR HER when Nina came down the wide marble stairs. Her swimsuit matched Cassandra's tube dress too well to be a coincidence. The deep blue fabric—accentuating Cassandra's curves—even shared the same decorations as Nina's swimwear. It made for an alluring combination. The short dress still had some elegance to it, while Nina's one-piece was downright sexy—her nipples poked prominently through the thin fabric.

Cassandra smirked, once again eyeing Nina up and down without shame before dragging her outside by her wrist. "Come on, I'm late for a meeting, so this is your first assignment."

Nina gasped as she got roughly yanked along, reminding her that—despite Cassandra's beauty and needs—the billionaire was still an entitled brat. Nina followed through the courtyard to the parked cars. Her dusty old sedan looked comically out of place, but she stopped smiling when Cassandra remotely opened the large, swinging doors of the Batmobile-like coupe.

"Uh, hold on." Nina fought Cassandra's insistent pulling. "You don't expect me to drive that, do you?"

Cassandra turned and frowned. "You do realize that you work for me?"

"I've never been in anything like that."

"You're okay with going down in a restroom, and eating ass like you love it," Cassandra crossed her arms, "but you're drawing the line at driving?"

"It costs more than I'll ever make!" Nina blurted out, waving at the supercar.

Cassandra ran her hand over Nina's shoulder. "Maybe not anymore, pet. At least, if you grow a pair and get behind the wheel, already."

Cassandra lowered herself into the passenger seat, leaving Nina to decide. She wasn't all that confident about driving this weird thing with the funny name. She recalled the video she skimmed through—even the reviewer considered it insanity on wheels. And yet, Cassandra seemed convinced Nina would conquer her doubts. That faith powered Nina through her fear.

Nina failed to mimic Cassandra's elegance as she worked her way down into the low seat, putting her in the cockpit of what might as well have been a spaceship. Cassandra scolded her when she reached for the door, which had swung out and upward but showed no handle to close it with. *I should've watched the whole video.*

"You'll need to figure some of this out." Cassandra snapped her fingers to draw Nina's gaze to the large touchscreen on the dashboard. A tap on the door-shaped icons made the heavy doors slide back down with a soft thud.

"It took Dora ten minutes to even start this thing." Cassandra pressed a button above them, near the windshield. The humming and soft grumbling sounded nothing like Nina's car, but also unlike any supercar she had ever seen up close.

"Wait," Nina turned to face her boss as she put on her seatbelt, "why don't you drive?"

"I failed the exam like six times before I gave up." Cassandra shrugged. "Even tried to bribe them, but that didn't work."

Nina scoffed. "All that money…"

"Fuck you." Cassandra slapped her. It was only a playful strike, but her words carried the most emotion she had shown Nina so far—when she wasn't having an orgasm, anyway.

"I'm sorry," Nina said, figuring out how to adjust the seat with the touchscreen—while stroking her tingling cheek. The number of options only made it harder to settle for a comfortable position. At least she didn't have to worry about the mirrors —they were all cameras.

Cassandra tapped her phone, causing the gate of her walled-off courtyard to open. She waved her hand dismissively. "Go on. I did mention I was late, didn't I?"

Nina took a few sharp breaths to work up the courage of driving the otherworldly car—and to keep herself from addressing Cassandra's attitude. When she pressed the gas pedal, the beast roared but didn't move. She mumbled an excuse and an expletive, looking at the steering wheel to find a stalk or something.

"You're sure *you* have a license?" Cassandra shook her head. Her smile betrayed her attempt at belittling Nina.

"Yeah, yeah." Nina tugged on a handle with a plus sign. The tiny screen on top of the wheel showed a big D. "There we go. I don't drive a crazy egg every day."

"Koenigsegg," Cassandra corrected. She held on to the dashboard when Nina pressed the accelerator far too much, sending them across the courtyard in a split second before Nina found the brake.

"Motherfucker," she groaned as the supercar stopped in an instant.

"Just take it easy." Cassandra put her hand on Nina's leg, making it all the harder to follow that advice.

"No shit." Nina gripped the wheel so hard it turned her knuckles white. She inched her foot off the brake, sighing as the powerful car now crawled away. *It's just a car.* As she steered to the open road ahead, she tapped the accelerator with her toes. The humming increased as the speed did. *See? Not so bad.*

When Nina came here, the view of the lake and Cassandra's mansion were a wonderful sight to behold, but now she only had one thing in mind—not crashing into the dirt.

"Don't be tense." Cassandra squeezed the blonde's leg, startling her. "You're stressing me out when you look like that."

"Shut up," Nina said, looking left and right half a dozen times as she arrived at the intersection. "You want to get there alive?"

"Mind your manners, pet." Cassandra moved her hand up Nina's thigh. "You don't want to test me."

For someone who seemed so classy, Cassandra sure was naughty. Nina tried to angle her leg away as she braked, still getting used to how directly the car reacted to her feet. The heels didn't make it any easier, nor did Cassandra's teasing fingers. They tested her resolve, nearing the edge of the swimsuit and groping her like a needy teenager.

Even though she had plenty of room to merge onto the main road, Nina waited until the handful of cars passed before creeping along. She giggled at the way the speedometer kept upright on the wheel-mounted screen as she turned, but when she pointed at it with a childish grin, Cassandra just shook her head.

"Walking would be faster," Cassandra said. She chuckled at Nina's groaning response.

Nina took a deep breath before fighting her reluctance. With the wide open road empty ahead, she rolled her shoulders and hit the gas. Cassandra's scream matched Nina's as the powerful egg shot forward, turning thirty miles an hour into sixty, ninety...

It took but a moment to catch up with the cars she had waited for at the intersection, the engine whining otherworldly as Nina let go of the accelerator.

"Jesus, what do you feed this thing?" she asked, overtaking the car in front without needing to work for it. "Blood of virgins?"

"Ask Leslie," Cassandra said, her voice straining as Nina hit the gas again. "All I know is, she's fast."

Fast was an understatement. They zoomed past the other drivers in a comfort Nina's car couldn't even match when parked. The expensive exterior muffled the odd sounds of the engine along with the wind noise, making it surreal to see the law-breaking speeds on the screen.

"It's all or nothing with you, isn't it?" Cassandra clutched the oh shit handle. Nina took the hint, even if she enjoyed not having Cassandra's hands tease her legs for a moment. While she backed off to a more acceptable speed, she glanced at her lover briefly. In that moment, seeing that smile on Cassandra's face, Nina finally accepted it all. Here she was, flying down the road in a car few people could afford, sitting next to the most beautiful woman on the planet. If this wasn't heaven, she couldn't imagine what would be even better. *Other than hearing her say "I love you"*.

Perhaps Cassandra noticed Nina's revelation. She played with Nina's hair. "Glad you said yes?"

Nina let out a laughing sigh, growing increasingly more comfortable with Cassandra and the absurd car.

"I don't think I've actually said yes, yet." Nina bit her lip.

Cassandra leaned in to kiss Nina's cheek. "Oh, but your tongue did."

Defending Her

CHAPTER 9

Nina kept her eyes glued on the city roads despite Cassandra's exploring hands. Even when there was enough space, she stressed out about hitting something. When the navigation announced the last turn, Nina sighed in relief. Parking the weird car proved to be another challenge, but she did what she assumed Cassandra would do. Nina stopped right near the entrance of the skyscraper as if she owned the place. Cassandra's chuckle confirmed she had the right idea.

As extravagant as it was, watching the Koenigsegg's immense doors open with a soft hiss put a smile on Nina's face. It was over the top—the entire car was—but the creators certainly didn't half-ass the splendor of the supercar.

Nina wasn't as graceful as Cassandra in getting out, and she got a little flustered when a bunch of people recorded them—recorded *her*—with their phones. This was her new life, driving exotic cars in a swimsuit. She bit her lip as Cassandra held out her hand, rushing around the car to accept it. Though wearing a gorgeous, skimpy one-piece in public made Nina a little giddy, the fact Cassandra deemed her a good enough trophy drove her pride well above her shyness. Their matching outfits only reinforced Nina's feelings. *We belong together.*

Nina pranced alongside Cassandra as they entered the building, holding her head up high. While the two doormen hid their emotions well, some businessmen inside threw glares of envy and judgment. A young man, barely eighteen by the looks of it, blushed as he guided Nina and Cassandra into the elevator without speaking. He knew their destination, and his bowed head suggested he knew who Cassandra was. Nina smiled. *That's right, cower before her.*

"You handled that pretty well, pet." Cassandra slapped Nina's ass. The teenage host coughed. Nina couldn't blame the boy for failing to keep quiet—they were quite the couple. Simply being around Cassandra strengthened her heart. Before meeting her, Nina would never have worn a swimsuit like this to the beach—let alone to an office. But Cassandra's powerful presence made her brave.

Cassandra didn't let go of Nina's hand for so much as a second. Nina didn't plan on letting her master go, either, squeezing Cassandra's hand. They got out of the elevator on the top floor, where their host left them in the care of a chubby woman in a form-fitting suit. She welcomed Cassandra by name and winked at Nina—who lowered her eyes for a moment before reminding herself to be in control. *Like Cassandra.* Nina beamed as her boss introduced her to Rachel, Cassandra's secretary. The flawless, dark skin made it hard to estimate her age

—she could've been in her early thirties or well past fifty.

"They're throwing a fit, as always." Rachel tapped her earpiece as the girls followed her to the meeting room. "What else is new?"

Cassandra chuckled. She didn't seem concerned. Nina joined her in the large office overlooking the sprawling city from a few hundred feet up high. Nothing here was subtle. Whatever business took place on this floor involved more money than Nina could count.

The four men and two women were exactly like the people Nina wouldn't want anything to do with. Dressed in suits as bland and expressionless as their faces, every single one of them sucked the life out of the room. Cassandra's grip tightened—she shared Nina's opinion.

"Miss Cardona, how nice of you to join us," the oldest of the women said. She obviously didn't mean it.

The group's emotionless attitude fueled Nina's need to display Cassandra's importance—even if she knew nothing about her lady's role. She let go of Cassandra's hand to pull back a chair—the chair at the head of the table, where she deemed the billionaire needed to be. Cassandra smiled as she sat down. Nina took place next to her, following a trend of taking rather than asking.

"Well then," Cassandra put her hands on the table, "care to explain why you dragged me all the way out here?"

To become her best aide, Nina hid her ignorance of the whole situation behind an attempt at a resting bitch face. While she could never compare to Cassandra's mean look, she tried to show a similar attitude. Two of the men, identical with their uninspired, short hairstyles, couldn't keep their eyes off Nina. She glared at them one at a time until they averted their gazes. It was like Cassandra's attitude rubbed off on her just by being close to her.

"Cassandra, I'll be blunt." One of the other men put a folder of paperwork on the table. His arrogance already hit Nina the wrong way. *Don't disrespect my woman.* The man adjusted his glasses as he took a quick look at his reports. "You're spending a lot of money. Cardona money."

Cassandra didn't respond, and Nina kept her thoughts to herself. *That's what it's there for, isn't it?* The stiff people looked like they had enough money to enjoy themselves—but chose not to. Too rich not to understand how well-off they were, too unimaginative to make the best of it.

"Just because you're the heiress to lady Catherine Cardona," the man said, "doesn't mean you can just throw it all away."

Though she had promised herself to stay silent, Nina snorted. *So, even when you're filthy rich, some people will meddle in your life every chance they get.*

"Actually, John, that's exactly what it means," Cassandra spoke the man's name as if she tasted something foul. Nina shook her head upon hearing it. He looked like a John, and not in a good way.

"We're not saying you can't enjoy yourself." The woman across the table cleared her throat as she took the paperwork from John. "But you're taking company money to fly around the world."

Nina raised her eyebrows. That didn't sound so bad. She could see herself following Cassandra all around the globe. Her smile probably ticked these people off even more.

"Well, Theresa," Cassandra said, "if you would invest the fortune the way mama told you, there'd be more coming in every year than even I can spend all my life."

Cassandra admitted her lavish lifestyle, at least. While Nina was in no position to judge the expenses, she took Cassandra's side.

"Let us worry about how to invest," the young guy on the left said. "You just worry about not spending everything your family has built for five generations."

"Hah!" Nina blurted out, unable to abide the annoying inquisition. "Listen to yourself. You're whining about her, while your very existence depends on her money."

These suits made her blood boil. Calling out her Cassandra like that? *No way.*

"Listen, miss…" the youngest of the men shuffled in his seat.

"No, you listen." She got up and leaned on the table, ignoring the fact she was a swimsuit-wearing servant in a room with dull businesspeople. "Do you think Catherine pays you to sit around and moan about her daughter? Huh?"

She surprised herself with these words, but the sinking shoulders and mumbles confirmed what Nina assumed. *Everyone's afraid of the head of the family.*

"That's right," she said. "All of you are here because of the Cardona family. Don't you dare forget that."

Only the eldest woman had a sense of defiance, careful as it was. "We are just concerned for the family's future. Cassandra—"

"Miss Cardona," Nina snarled. Her heart surged with adrenaline.

"Miss Cardona," the woman corrected herself, "simple spends more than the family can afford in the long run."

Simply. Nina chuckled. *It's never simple.* They had to be overreacting. Wasn't Cassandra a billionaire? Nobody could spend that much to get into financial trouble. She beckoned the woman to hand over the reports.

"Holy shit." Nina needed to sit back down when she saw all the big numbers—just from January. "That's an expensive boat."

Cassandra shrugged. "It's not like I buy one every year."

"Actually..." One of the young men raised his finger. He didn't finish his objection. It wouldn't even surprise Nina if the billionaire had multiple yachts. She shook her head. *That's not the point.*

"Okay, I mean, she's not frugal," Nina flipped through the pages, noticing one million-dollar purchase after another. "But let's be frank. How much do we have in the bank?"

Cassandra chuckled. Nina paid her no mind, focusing on her honor now.

Theresa said, "Well, Cassa—Miss Cardona's net worth is around 7.6 billion."

Nina blinked. Only now did her former self take over for a bit. *Seven point six billion. Jesus.* Nina recently hit the end of the month with little under seven dollars. She couldn't picture what seven *billion* dollars looked like.

"But," Theresa spoke carefully, "it was 8.2 billion last year."

Nina's nervous laughter broke her character. She wasn't much of a financial wonder, but that seemed like a pretty steep drop. Cassandra remained unbothered throughout it all. She let her pet run loose, and Nina had a bark she wasn't aware of until now.

"Look, I get it." She put the absurd bank statements down. "It seems excessive. But have you ever driven a curling egg? Because I have, and once you get used to that lifestyle, there's no going back."

One man rubbed his forehead. They didn't approve of this. *Perhaps it's my outfit.* Being told to shove it by a girl in a swimsuit probably damaged their egos. But they came after Cassandra—Nina couldn't let that slide.

"Bottom line," Cassandra finally spoke up, "you just have to make us more money. I don't need to involve mom in this, right?"

"No, miss Cardona," half of the group mumbled in unison. The remaining few followed—after being called out one by one.

Cassandra rose, and Nina followed. She took her lover's hand as they left the room together, Nina smirking at the brattiness she copied from Cassandra. Rachel laughed as the girls approached.

"Girl, you're a perfect fit for Cassie," Rachel said. "I think she has finally found the one."

While Cassandra didn't reward her with a confirmation, Nina took the lack of denial as a win. *You don't have to tell me.* Nina couldn't believe what they just went through. *Why did I defend her?* The spoiled, bratty billionaire didn't deserve Nina's pity. And yet...

"That piece looks *so* good on you, by the way." Rachel stroked Nina's bare arms. "You'll be making headlines soon, I'm sure!"

Nina gulped. That hadn't even crossed her mind, even after the small crowd taking pictures outside. She used to live in a different world. One where the name Cassandra Cardona meant nothing. She put it out of her mind and smiled at Rachel. "Thanks. I'm just glad to be by her side."

It was no lie or exaggeration. Cassandra attracted her, even if Nina couldn't pinpoint why. The brat tried to keep her distance one minute, then appeared to open up the next. Nina had no idea what to expect from her boss and lover, but her feelings became harder to ignore.

"Thank you, as always." Cassandra kissed Rachel on the cheek before guiding Nina back to the elevator. As the door closed, she threw Nina against the wall, who stared back with widened eyes.

"What was that?" Cassandra came up close, really close. Nina trembled as she felt the breath on her face. Cassandra's stern look didn't last. After a few moments, the corners of her lips twitched until she grinned. "Nobody has ever defended me like that."

Nina thought of things to say, but her mind stopped working when Cassandra made that much-wanted move—kissing Nina on the mouth. As the slight touch sent jolts through Nina's body, she parted her lips to welcome her lover. *Oh, Cass!*

Cassandra's hands came to Nina's face and neck, stroking her with frantic excitement more befitting a schoolgirl. Nina closed her eyes and hummed, her hands running up Cassandra's side to her shoulders. Cassandra pressed herself against Nina as they aggressively French kissed, driven by pent-up desire. She broke the kiss only to pepper Nina's nose with affection.

"Don't leave me," Cassandra licked Nina's cheek. "Promise to stay with me."

Nina's heart fluttered at the desperation in Cassandra's voice. Yachts, cars, mansions. None of it mattered, not to either of them. At last, Cassandra made that clear to Nina, who had felt that way from their first encounter. She shoved Cassandra back just far enough to hold her face and stare her in the eyes. "I'm not going anywhere."

Those words were all it took. Cassandra's eyes lit up. She pushed herself against Nina again, careless that her lover's fingers made a mess of her hair. Nina's surrender had been clear from the start, but the butterflies in her stomach fluttered now that Cassandra expressed her love as well. Maybe it all happened too fast. She didn't care. With Cassandra's plush lips on hers, Nina needed nothing else. She didn't so much as glance at the opening door when they reached the ground floor. Cassandra just spun her around and crashed her against the other wall so she could reach for the button that closed the door again.

"Oh, Cass." Nina inched back and cupped Cassandra's face. "I think I love you."

She moved to kiss again, but Cassandra put her finger on Nina's lips.

"You think?" Cassandra teased by kissing her finger between their mouths. When the doors opened again, she slammed the console until she hit the emergency stop button. The ringing didn't distract them. Nina pulled Cassandra's hand aside, diving back in. She gave her answer without words, holding on to Cassandra's shoulders. They giggled when a voice outside interrupted their fun.

"Everything all right in there?" A man asked. They didn't answer. Cassandra's grin removed Nina's inhibitions. She lowered through her knees to kiss Cassandra's collarbone and down between her tits, hoping she'd leave a trail of her expensive lipstick. As possessive as Cassandra was, Nina's desires grew to mark her girlfriend as well. She paused for a moment.

"Are we girlfriends?" Nina glanced up at Cassandra before sliding the thin dress aside. She didn't wait for an answer even if she prayed for confirmation, flicking her tongue over Cassandra's nipple and wrapping her lips around it.

"If that's what you want..." Cassandra's soft voice barely peaked over the noisy alarm, but the way her hand rested on Nina's head said more than enough. Nina sucked on Cassandra's nipple, nibbling it just enough to startle her lover.

"I do want that," Nina said as she moved even lower, kissing Cassandra's belly. "And I want you to say it."

"If I don't?" Cassandra wrapped Nina's hair in her hand.

"Just say it. Please."

The elevator doors opened with a loud clunk, startling Nina. Cassandra pulled her up to her feet and adjusted her dress before anyone came into view. They smiled sheepishly at the teenager who guided them earlier.

Annoyed at the interruption, Nina groaned as Cassandra once again dragged her around like a toy. She came this close to having her lover admit undeniable feelings. Even though they were just words,

Nina needed to hear them. She needed to hear Cassandra admit her love.

The small crowd outside had diminished further, leaving only a handful of people focusing on the mad supercar. Just a few of them turned their attention to Nina in her swimsuit and Cassandra in the matching skimpy dress. It was enough of an audience to startle Nina, however, when Cassandra yanked her into a tight embrace to kiss her again. Nina's eyes widened, and she teared up a little. Showing her off like a trophy was one thing—a kiss told the world a lot more. A kiss told the world everything.

Cassandra took Nina's chin, kissed her nose, and said, "Nina, you *are* my girlfriend."

Nina stroked Cassandra's arms. "I thought you—"

"Shut up." Cassandra planted a quick kiss on Nina's lips. "I'm sick of running."

The surrounding murmurs became background noise for Nina. Her dizzy mind barely comprehended Cassandra's confession. She caressed her girlfriend's face and gazed into the dark eyes. *Girlfriend.* These dark eyes were no longer bratty or dominant. They filled up with the adoration of a puppy. Nina beamed at Cassandra and embraced her with no intention of ever letting go.

"Take me home." Cassandra kissed Nina's neck. "Before I fuck you right here."

"You wouldn't."

Cassandra squeezed Nina's ass, leaving the barely covered cheek red, and Nina flustered. It took a lot of effort to break the hug. Even when she did, Nina sneaked in one last kiss on Cassandra's mouth. The bystanders filmed and commented, but Nina ignored them all in her love-struck haze as she hurried to get into the car. She gazed at her girlfriend beside her and drove off—drove *home*.

Coming Home

CHAPTER 10

Nina hurried to get out of the car and back into Cassandra's arms. They left the exotic car as it was—doors open and engine running—to rush inside, stumbling and giggling in each other's arms.

"Are you sure about this?" Nina bit Cassandra's lip. Now that the time was right, she took it all the way. *You're mine as much as I am yours.*

Cassandra tipped over an ugly vase as she spun Nina around against the wall. The shattering of ceramic on marble made Nina jump, but it also answered her question. They giggled as Cassandra's hands roamed Nina's body, stroking her arms and cupping her breasts. Nina swooned in her girlfriend's embrace. *Girlfriend. Finally.* Though it had just been a few days, Cassandra's surrender had taken too long for Nina. And yet, it made the payoff even sweeter.

"I'm sorry I doubted you." Cassandra sucked Nina's lower lip and pushed her toward the stairs. They tripped as they went up, Cassandra landing on Nina on the carpeted floor. Pausing only to admire

Cassandra's lovable face, Nina admired her billionaire girlfriend's doting expression. She showed the real Cassandra now—the one that yearned for love as much as Nina did. Nina pulled her in and smooched her, content to just have sex in the foyer. But Cassandra kicked off her heels and backed away. She got to her feet and dragged Nina up along with her.

"Bedroom!" Cassandra wrapped her arms around Nina's back, urging her up the stairs, then into the left hallway. Nina struggled to get rid of her stilettos as well, leaving the thousand-dollar heels behind them as she squeezed Cassandra's ass. She peppered her girlfriend's neck with kisses and almost lost her footing again.

"Wait." Cassandra tugged on Nina's hair. "We'll never get to my room like this."

Nina pulled Cassandra in by her nape, pressing her face against her neck. "Your fault for living in a place this big."

"Too late to complain," Cassandra said. "You like it here. I know you do."

She held her hands out behind her to guide herself along the wall while Nina hugged her tight, working her lips and tongue over Cassandra's neck.

"I love how you stood up for me." Cassandra giggled. She kicked the door to her bedroom. "You're so sexy when you're protective."

"I'm always sexy," Nina said as Cassandra threw her onto the bed with a possessive smirk. Nina didn't care about being arrogant now—she earned that right. "It's why you begged me to live with you."

"I begged you, hmm?" Cassandra cocked her head. She slid one strap of her dress down her shoulder, teasing her lover with her perfect body.

"I'm glad you agree." Nina crawled back on the enormous bed. She yanked her swimsuit down her body. Expensive as it was, it just got in the way now. She bit her lip as she teased her stiff nipples, watching Cassandra strip out of the elegant black dress. As stunning as Cassandra was in her luxurious dresses, nothing could make her prettier than her natural form.

"You were pretty eager to accept." Cassandra trailed a finger from her lips, down her neck, and over her flat belly. If she tried to regain control, she failed when Nina parted her legs and winked.

"Your turn." Nina squeezed her tits. "You've teased me enough."

Cassandra's eyes fixated on her sex, driving Nina wild. Everything had been about her submission— now Cassandra's deep desires surfaced. Desires for Nina. Cassandra crawled onto the bed, inching closer while Nina spread her legs wider. Her eager arousal filled her nostrils. "You're so hot."

Cassandra hummed, kissing her way up Nina's leg from her ankle without taking her eyes off her goal. Nina's breaths quickened the further up her girlfriend kissed, the anticipation nearly enough to send her over the edge. She held her breath when Cassandra's lips left her inner thigh and brushed over her labia.

"Oh, Cass." Nina gripped the bedsheets as she gawked at her lover between her legs. Cassandra winked. Was she ever this pretty? She planted a single, overwhelming kiss. Nina didn't so much as blink as she stared at Cassandra. "Please…"

Their earlier encounters had been one-sided, even if Nina got off on that dynamic. Now it was all about her, Cassandra taking her time the way Nina had done before. Warm breath on her lips. A gentle lick around her clit. Cassandra's hands pinned her legs down when Nina's thighs trembled. Propped on her elbows, Nina stared down over her heaving breasts, imploring her girlfriend for more.

"Is this what you want?" Cassandra winked before kissing Nina's lips—just a light touch to toy with her.

"Come on," Nina took a ragged breath, "stop fucking around."

Her legs struggled against Cassandra's hands. If she wanted to, Nina could just grab Cassandra's head and force her in...but the teasing made her heart flutter. She never felt this way about anyone before.

The moment Cassandra dove in, Nina's arms gave out. Cassandra's tongue parting her lips to wiggle inside made Nina swoon. She closed her eyes and opened her soul, crying out her girlfriend's name. Cassandra did her part, bringing a thumb to Nina's clit while mimicking the lewd kissing of their first meeting. Nina smiled as her mind brought her back there—back to the restroom. Where she surrendered herself to go down on a stranger. She recalled all too well how Cassandra stared down at her. Possessively. Now that same filthy billionaire twirled her tongue in Nina's tight pussy while rubbing her clit. Cassandra was a spoiled, entitled brat...just not for Nina. Not anymore. More than just sex, Cassandra going down on Nina proved her love.

Nina gasped when Cassandra's tongue went from her soaking wet pussy to her throbbing clit.

"Oh, Cass!" Nina's hands shot to her girlfriend's head, grabbing her hair and pulling her away—just to pull her close again. She was too sensitive to suffer Cassandra's lips on her clit, but far too aroused to do without it. Whimpers left her mouth as Cassandra flicked her tongue the same way Nina had done to her. Cassandra slid a finger into Nina's pussy, and her muscles clamped down around her knuckle. With one thigh no longer held down, Nina threw her leg over Cassandra's back to hold her tight.

"Oh shit, oh fuck." Nina thrashed on the bed, tightening her grip on Cassandra's head. She feared hurting her girlfriend, but she couldn't stop herself. "Sorry, sorry!"

Cassandra responded by sucking on her clit. Nina cried out in bliss as jolts of pleasure shot through her body from her overstimulated pussy. Her whole body spasmed and jerked against Cassandra's assault. She tried to push her lover away, unable to take it all, but Cassandra sealed herself on Nina's clit. The rough love was the most effective payback for Nina's earlier encounters. Her eyes rolled back, her heart hammered in her chest, and she held on to Cassandra's head for dear life.

Nina's back arched as she threw herself onto her side, clenching Cassandra between her thighs and riding her face even as she tried to break away at the same time. Cassandra's unrelenting kissing and sucking brought Nina to the verge of passing out. She became lightheaded and stopped breathing altogether, her mind incapable of handling it all.

Even when Cassandra ceased licking her clit, Nina couldn't unwrap her thighs from around her girlfriend's head. As her muscles tightened up, Cassandra had to pry herself free from the vice grip, leaving Nina panting like a dog.

"Jesus, Nina." Cassandra kissed Nina's legs, back, and neck. "I didn't know you were that sensitive."

Nina couldn't speak. She barely even smiled when Cassandra rolled her onto her back and cuddled up against her. Nina cooed, opening her eyes just enough to look at Cassandra.

"I love you," Nina whispered as all her strength left her body.

Cassandra nibbled Nina's neck and cupped her breasts. "I know you do."

Nina stroked her lover—her girlfriend—as she let her exhaustion claim her, drifting asleep while Cassandra caressed her all over.

NINA WOKE UP IN CASSANDRA'S BED, under the covers now. She smiled back at her sweetheart, who lay on her side, gazing lovingly at her.

"I've never bored someone so much they fell asleep on me." Cassandra tapped Nina's nose.

"Oh, Cass," Nina whispered. "I had the most amazing dream about you."

"Really?" Cassandra worked herself on top of Nina. Her long, dark hair fell around their faces like a curtain.

"Yeah," Nina moved up to give a quick kiss, "you actually told me you love me. It was so sweet."

Cassandra chuckled. She welcomed her lover's lips, giving Nina a taste of herself.

"What a silly dream," Cassandra said. She put her hands beside Nina's head and slid up, straddling Nina's neck.

No matter how worn out she was, Nina couldn't pass the opportunity to taste Cassandra again. She held on to her girlfriend's thighs—to pull her closer. Cassandra shuffled forward, grinning down with lust. Her scent filled the air. The scent that enthralled Nina from their first moments together. Nina kissed the thick thighs as they worked their way onto her pillow, against her cheeks. Beautiful as Cassandra was from below, Nina much preferred to see the beautiful face. She didn't merely lust for the billionaire—she was head over heels in love.

"What about you?" Cassandra grasped Nina's hair. "Do you love me?"

Nina refused to answer. She wiggled downward when Cassandra stopped moving up, putting herself in the position to be smothered. Cassandra obliged, inching up just to make sure her pussy came to rest on Nina's lips. Nina's fingers dug into the warm, soft thighs threatening to take away her breath. She lapped Cassandra's pussy, kissing her lover's vulva with devotion.

While kneeling in submission had its perks, lying down like that put Nina in a spot she could remain in for hours—as long as Cassandra let her breathe sometimes. She guided her girlfriend, nudging her around to better worship her lips, clit, and ass alike. Cassandra giggled when Nina's tongue slathered her asshole, reminding both of them of the thrills Nina's asslicking provided.

"Oh, you dirty whore." Cassandra arched her back and pressed down, cutting off Nina's breath for a moment. It drove Nina to finger herself without shame, loving the insistent smothering more than anything. With Cassandra spreading her cheeks over her face, Nina smooched her girlfriend's sphincter with lewd smacks. Cassandra's weight forced her down into the pillow, suffocating her.

"Go on," Cassandra danced on Nina's mouth, "tongue my asshole, you filthy slut."

Though Nina could not be less ashamed of her submission, the words still made her flustered. She ran her slick fingers over her own asshole while probing Cassandra's pucker with her tongue. Her girlfriend's muscles relaxed easier than her own, but she worked a finger into her ass while tonguing Cassandra's.

"Fuck, yes," Cassandra hissed. "Eat my ass."

Nina arched her back as she thrashed under her girlfriend, fingering her ass and rubbing her clit. She struggled to breathe through her nose, smothered under Cassandra's divine body, but breathing came second to pleasure. Her slippery tongue earned her delightful giggles from her lover's mouth while pressing deeper down her own asshole. She only regretted that her tongue wasn't as long as her finger.

"Oh, keep going!" Cassandra slapped, rubbed, and kneaded her clit with a roughness matched by Nina's. As sensitive as they both were, they brought each other to an overwhelming climax. Nina's face hurt as her girlfriend rode her hard, and she struggled to keep up with her tongue. She used what little wiggle room she had to crane her neck, tonguing Cassandra's asshole even deeper. Even after Cassandra's heart-warming surrender, Nina's high washed over her once more. Breathless and dizzy with love, she pinched her clit, sending wave after wave of pleasure down her whole body. She moaned into

Cassandra's ass as she thrashed around on the bed, her back arched uncomfortably.

Cassandra cried out Nina's name as the spasming of her asshole massaged Nina's tongue. As the twitching sphincter clenched, Nina forced herself to stay with her lover despite the ever-increasing need for oxygen. Her throbbing clit eclipsed the desperate hammering of her heart—and the burning of her lungs.

Nina only got to breathe at the mercy of Cassandra, who threw herself back onto the bed beside her. Nina wheezed as she drew in fresh air. She glanced at Cassandra, still quivering in bliss, and clutched her hand. "That was amazing…"

They scrambled to get into each other's arms, giggling and smooching as their hands roamed their bodies. Even after their shared climax, the doting couple groped, stroked, and squeezed in a lustful embrace. Cassandra rolled back on top, where she belonged, kissing Nina's face all over.

"Can you please say it now?" Nina nuzzled her nose against her girlfriend's. "I know you want to."

Cassandra cupped Nina's chin and gazed into her eyes. She teased with silence for a while longer, her smirk growing bigger with each passing moment. Cassandra leaned in for another long, sloppy kiss before pulling away and speaking those magic words.

"I love you."

Hope for the Best

CHAPTER 11

Showing off wealth wasn't as fun as Nina expected. She was uncomfortable leaving the Koenigsegg parked out in the open. A bunch of people had already gathered around it while two guys kept filming her even as she entered the coffee shop. She triple-checked to make sure she locked the car before walking over to Hope. Her best friend sat in the usual place, with her back toward the entrance.

"Hey, you." Nina tapped Hope's shoulder, a little anxious about meeting up, despite Hope's role in motivating Nina to give Cassandra a shot.

"Nini!" Hope jumped up to hug Nina, taking away the unwarranted worries. "God, you're beaming. How are things going with Cassandra?"

Nina didn't know where to begin, so she admitted the best part with a shit-eating grin. "We're in love."

"I can see that!" Hope pulled out her phone. "Shit, a million people have seen it."

Nina blushed as Hope showed her the candid photos. She looked incredible in some of them—

104

strutting with pure confidence in the arms of Cassandra. Others showed the more wanton side of their relationship, with a useless red circle around the billionaire's hand squeezing her butt. Hope took the time to read a bunch of headlines, showering Nina with praises and insults.

"It's shocking how envious and hurtful people can be," Hope said after reading another demeaning line. She winked as she added, "Even if you *are* a gold digger."

Hope put her phone away and took Nina's hands, her expression serious and affectionate. "I'm so glad it's working out. Tell me everything!"

Nina ordered a few muffins from the barista, who gave her a knowing wink. Nina smiled back before turning to her best friend with a dreamy glint in her eyes. "Oh, Hope. Cass is such a handful. But I got through to her, and..."

"And?" Hope leaned in and rested her face on her hands. Her warm smile showed genuine happiness.

"I don't know. She's wound so tight in public, but she's different once you get close to her. I mean, two days ago she told me she only wanted me for, you know..."

"Sex," Hope said without blinking. "And now?"

"And now she loves me. She said it!" Nina glanced outside at the multi-million-dollar car, spotting a few kids getting a little too close to it for her liking. "Ah, damn it."

Hope turned to investigate. "Jesus. Is that yours?"

"Not to keep. I mean, unless I marry her, I guess?"

"Sure, why not," Hope kicked Nina's leg under the table, "you've already known each other for *days*."

Nina smiled at the barista, who put down a plate of muffins—the ones Hope loved so much.

"Look, believe me, I get it. It's stupid." Nina took a bite of the sweet chocolate muffin. "But I also don't want to let this opportunity pass me by. And not because of the money."

"Oh, no," Hope winked, "of course not. Who needs all that Versace in her life, right?"

Nina shrugged and ate her muffin. Sure, those luxurious dresses were adorable, and those heels...

"You best believe I'm going to call you a gold digger from now on." Hope took one of her favorite muffins as well. "With your Vuitton purse."

Nina stared at her friend, trying to figure out if she really didn't feel weird about the sudden and massive wealth difference.

"Don't give me that look." Hope munched down on the muffin. "Don't you fucking pity me."

"I'm not." Nina looked outside again, at the bunch of people ogling her car. One of them even leaned against it. "It's just awkward suddenly being so rich."

"You are paying for these muffins though," Hope said.

"Sure." Nina got up and put her hands on the table, a scowl forming on her face as she glared at the kids near her car. "I'll be right back."

She hurried outside on her expensive stilettos, shouting at the teenagers leaning against the Koenigsegg. "Hey, get off!"

One of them, a girl who appeared barely sixteen, slid off the hood and stepped up. "Yo, calm down, princess. We're just having fun."

"Yeah, well, don't." Nina crossed her arms, not sure what to say.

Another kid nodded at the expensive ride. "What is that, anyway?"

Nina took a deep breath. *Don't be so hard on them. They're just kids.* She told him about the Koenigsegg, hoping she'd get the pronunciation right. The oldest of the bunch, judging by his size, still leaned against it.

"How much cock you gotta suck to earn that?" He asked. His friends hollered at his childish question. Nina balled her fists, even if the boy wasn't far off the mark.

"Relax," he waved his hands, "I'm just messing with you. Seriously though, you must give epic head."

The pretentious laughs made Nina's blood boil— as did the fact the fat boy still touched the car.

"Playtime's over," Hope said as she stepped beside Nina. "Go be assholes elsewhere."

"Oh, I'm sorry," the younger girl said. Her voice dripped with sarcasm as she leaned against the car again as well. "Isn't this the land of the free?"

"Fine, have it your way," Nina muttered as she reached into her purse and held down the button on her phone—just as Jenny taught her. Everyone around her, Hope included, looked at her, dumbfounded. Maybe they expected her to pull out pepper spray or a knife. But they probably didn't expect the two blacked-out SUVs barreling down the parking lot, or the six men storming out with weapons drawn, yelling at everyone to stay still. Except for

Nina and Hope, who were ordered—and promptly dragged—to the back seats of one of the Cadillacs. Nina held Hope's hand throughout, reassuring her screaming friend it was all right. *They're my guys.*

HOPE WHEEZED INTO A BAG as they tumbled down the road at high speed while Nina tried to calm her down.

"It's okay, they're just—" Nina grunted as they hit a bump way over the speed limit. "They're following protocol."

The Koenigsegg trailed behind them, with one of the burly men at the wheel. They'd have to go back to pay for their coffee and muffins. Unless the guards had that covered as well. Jenny seemed like the type to have all of that worked out beforehand.

"Jesus, Nini." Hope waved her off. "You could have fucking warned me. I thought we were getting abducted."

Nina rubbed her friend's shoulders. She hadn't been prepared for it herself. Jenny might have told her things were well taken care of, but the speed and drama still came as a surprise. They didn't mess around when Cassandra's flock was in danger.

One of the big guys up front turned to face the two women. "Y'all okay back there?"

All the protectors appeared identical with black sunglasses, clothes, and hair. Minor differences in height and built aside, the team that swooped in and 'saved' the girls from the teenagers looked like mass-produced clones. They did their job more than admirably, however.

"Just a little rattled." Nina flashed a smile. "Thanks for reacting so fast."

"It's what we're here for, ma'am." He nodded, and a grin followed. "Never hesitate to call in the cavalry."

"Don't mind if I do," Nina said.

"One moment." The man tapped his earpiece. "Bravo here, go ahead."

He shook his head, suggesting impatience. After a few seconds, he winked at Nina as he addressed whoever was on the other end of the call. "Yup, Scimitar is safe. With a plus one."

The man rolled his eyes. "As you wish. Bravo, out."

"Drink up." He handed the girls a coke—and took one himself as well. "The sugar helps. Name's Travis, by the way."

"Nice to meet you," Nina opened one can and gave it to Hope. "Nina, but I'm sure you already knew that. The mouth-breather here is Hope. She's usually not so shaky."

"Eat shit." Hope huffed. But her hands still trembled when she took the drink.

"Just relax now," Travis said. "We're almost there."

NINA HELPED HOPE OUT OF THE CAR, unable to hide her prideful smile as her friend gawked at the enormous mansion. They couldn't speak even if they wanted to, with the overwhelming noise of the helicopter swooping in. Nina took Hope's hand and hurried her to the landing pad, watching Cassandra's private chopper touch down.

"Really?" Hope shouted in Nina's ear. "A bit excessive, don't you think?"

"She's a billionaire, Hope," Nina said. "Excessive is kind of her jam."

Cassandra just about leaped out of the helicopter the moment one guard opened the door. She stormed at Nina with surprising speed and zero elegance, throwing herself into Nina's arms. "Oh, Nina, my love. You scared me."

Nina welcomed the embrace and ran her hands over Cassandra's back, soothing her while smiling at Hope. "It's okay, I'm here. I'm safe."

She gave her girlfriend the time she needed while Adria—the pilot—introduced herself to Hope and brought her inside. Nina and Cassandra held each other tight but didn't speak. Nina required nothing more than Cassandra's warmth. Judging by the way Cassandra's fingers gripped Nina's hair, the desire was mutual.

"I'm sorry for startling you," Nina whispered, now that the helicopter quieted down. "It was so silly. These fucking kids giving me shit just for—"

"I know, my love." Cassandra kissed her neck. "I know. It's all right."

Nina nuzzled against her girlfriend's face, savoring the sweet scent of Cassandra's hair. "I'm still shaking."

"Not as much as last night," Cassandra said. "Or this morning."

"You're relentless. Come on, I want you to meet Hope."

"Ah. The one who told me to fuck off." Cassandra squeezed Nina's hand to emphasize she joked.

"Hey, if it wasn't for her, you wouldn't have me." Nina entered the mansion hand-in-hand with her girlfriend. While they looked for Hope, she wondered if she would ever get used to the maze of the modern palace. They bumped into Adria, who said she left the guest in the library.

"Oh, for fuck's sake," Nina grunted. "That's all the way on the other side!"

Cassandra responded only with a chuckle. The two lovers turned back to go around the courtyard —taking a good four minutes to reach the west side of the mansion.

When they arrived, Hope had calmed down somewhat. She now gawked at all the books in the tidy library. Cassandra stepped away from Nina to introduce herself. "Hope, it's nice to properly meet you. I'm Cassandra Cardona."

"Properly?" Hope snorted as she shook Cassandra's hand. "Getting tossed into a black SUV by a bunch of hunks and seeing you get flown in by helicopter isn't exactly a proper introduction."

Cassandra shrugged. Hope always spoke her mind, often with an obvious grin. She didn't let go of Cassandra—instead pulling her into a quick hug.

"I don't know what to make of this," Hope said, "but my Nini loves you."

"Nini," Cassandra repeated as she turned to wink at Nina. "That's cute."

"You're really something." Hope cocked her head as she inspected Cassandra from top to bottom. Nina's girlfriend didn't seem to mind at all.

"Well, now that you're here," Cassandra waved toward the door, "how about lunch?"

"Hell, yeah," Hope said, taking the invitation without pause. She stepped into the hallway and looked around. "Where to?"

WATCHING CASSANDRA AND HOPE TOGETHER warmed Nina's heart. She just gazed at them in silence while the two got to know each other better. Her earlier fears of Hope disapproving of the wealthy woman proved unfounded—they got along surprisingly well.

"So, you want to own a bar?" Cassandra handed Hope a sandwich. "What's keeping you?"

"Money, Cassandra. It doesn't grow on trees for all of us." Hope stuffed her face with her lunch. "And a business degree, I suppose."

While Hope wasn't big on manners, Cassandra seemed to enjoy such openness. Most of the staff wasn't pretentious, which might have rubbed off on Cassandra over the years. At least in private. She asked Hope if she had any substantial plans yet.

"Oh, you're in for it now." Nina got up. "I hope you have the afternoon off to listen to her plans."

Hope scowled at her. But she also reached for her phone, proving Nina right—she kept her thorough business ideas with her at all times. As much as she teased her friend about it, Nina expected Hope's dreams to come true, if only for her sheer passion for the project.

"I'm gonna say hi to Jenny and thank her team." Nina kissed her girlfriend's cheek before walking off. "And, uh, I'm glad you two are getting along."

"Why wouldn't we?" both of them blurted out, then giggled.

Nina had a bounce in her step as she left her friend with her girlfriend. Everything fell into place. Hope and Cassandra accepting each other was the last piece of Nina's puzzle. With the shock of the parking lot incident wearing off, Nina's heart swelled with joy. For the first time in years, she felt unburdened. Complete. And, more importantly, loved.

Prancing Horse

CHAPTER 12

In contrast to Cassandra's earlier reluctance, she took the relationship to eleven now that the cat was out of the bag. Cassandra had surprised Nina with a simple text message. *Dinner at eight.* It wasn't a question, nor did it need to be. Scarlett had been adamant about giving Nina a full makeover for her first official date, so Nina spent all afternoon under the professional care of the excited makeup artist.

"It's a shame I'm dolling you up so nice," Scarlett said as she put the finishing touches to Nina's elaborate braids. "When you two are just going to ruin it all tonight, anyway."

Scarlett turned Nina into a queen with her extraordinary skills. Nina couldn't stop smiling at her mirror image. "If it were up to me, I'd look like this forever. You're incredible at this!"

"You're too sweet." Scarlett added a little more gloss to Nina's lips. "But you're a beautiful canvas to work with."

Nina couldn't wait to show herself to Cassandra. Though she loved herself the way she was, the only thing keeping her from becoming addicted to makeup was the price. Well, not anymore. Scarlett enjoyed her work so much that she insisted Nina came back whenever she wanted. Nina planned to take her up on that offer—a lot.

She almost cried at the gorgeous result of Scarlett's touch. The sparkly gold eyeshadow matched the glittery accents on her black dress, while the winged eyeliner made her bright blue eyes stand out more. Scarlett worked her magic well, sharpening Nina's cheekbones and coating her lips in a glossy gradient. Every single part of the art was pretty, but it combined to turn Nina into an absolute goddess— who couldn't wait to try out even more of Scarlett's transformations.

Cassandra beamed as she came into Scarlett's studio. She planted a firm, brief kiss on Scarlett's cheek and a more intense one on Nina's lips. "You look absolutely stunning."

"Thank you!" Nina bounced with excitement. "You don't look half-bad yourself."

Cassandra's recent declaration of love filled Nina's bravery and confidence. Although such a joke wouldn't have crossed her mind before, she no longer doubted the bond they had. Now she could open up her heart, unburdened by anxiety.

Cassandra's eyes darted around, admiring Nina's face up close—with a hint of depravity. Nina believed she didn't *need* the excessive makeup, but their first official date justified showing off. The desire in Cassandra's eyes made Nina more than a little flustered. Cassandra's thumb grazed her cheeks, and

Scarlett chuckled when the star-crossed women embraced in a long, sweet kiss.

"Ready, dear?" Cassandra asked. Nina nodded right away. Cassandra reached into her purse as she kneeled. "Lift your dress."

Nina nearly sank to her knees. *Now...?* Her eyes widened as she looked down at her girlfriend. Cassandra smirked, holding an obvious sex toy in her hand. Nina recognized it for what it was—a remote-controlled vibrator. Without further commands, she pulled up her short, sparkling dress with trembling fingers.

"No panties?" Cassandra pursed her lips. "Slut."

Nina gulped. Scarlett had assured her that's how Cassandra liked it. Nina glared at her stylist. *You better be right.* Scarlett winked. She wished the naughty lovebirds an amazing evening before leaving them to their games. They both responded with a hum, too focused on each other.

When Cassandra moved forward to kiss her thigh, Nina had to fight every instinct to let go of the dress and grab her lover's head. That one kiss already broke her down, but when Cassandra's fingers touched her labia, Nina trembled and whimpered.

"What are you doing?" Nina's newfound bravery disappeared when Cassandra coated the egg vibrator with lubrication.

"Don't play coy, pet." Cassandra ran her finger over Nina's labia before wiggling between them. "You know what this is."

While the pet name no longer hit Nina as hard now that she knew Cassandra's true feelings, the toy proved Cassandra still had a dominant streak.

"You almost gave me a heart attack today," Cassandra said while shoving the vibrator inside Nina's pussy. "This will be your punishment."

Nina cooed as her pussy welcomed the slippery insertion. If this was just the setup, she feared for what was to come—and how hard she was going to come.

"It's unfair." Nina whimpered. "I felt threatened. What else was I supposed to do?"

"They were kids, Nini," Cassandra said, using Hope's silly nickname. She pressed the toy deep inside Nina's vagina. "If you're going to raise the alarm for each tiny insult, you'll scare me every day."

"I didn't know you cared so much," Nina said. Cassandra punished her taunt by activating the vibrator with her phone. The gentle buzzing shut her defiance down.

"Oh, fuck!" Nina's hands shot down to her pussy, but Cassandra grabbed her wrists.

"Now, if you convince me you're sorry for startling me so," Cassandra lowered the vibrator's rhythm to a barely noticeable hum, "I'll make it easy for you."

Nina groaned but didn't speak up. *I won't give in so easily!*

"No?" Cassandra got to her feet and pulled Nina's dress back down. She stared into Nina's eyes. The toy in Nina's pussy vibrated even more intensely for a moment, drawing out another whimper.

"This will be a fun first date, then!" Cassandra's cruel laugh made Nina's heart flutter. *Uh oh.* With the vibrator snug inside her, and her face fiery red despite all the makeup, Nina bowed her head. Cassandra took her hand and smiled. "Let's go, my sweet."

As much as Nina feared the naughty plans, her heart surged with pride. Whatever sinful thrills Nina would have to endure, Cassandra made one thing very clear—they belonged together. Nina wasn't just a trophy to be fucked. Cassandra loved her. Everything else was background noise to that warmth—for now.

WITH HER LUXURIOUS LOVER AT HER SIDE, Nina fumbled with her phone to open the car app. She groaned when she saw the Koenigsegg unavailable. She had grown quite fond of it already, despite the crap the teenagers gave her for driving it.

Cassandra nudged Nina's shoulder. "We're taking the Ferrari."

"Which one?" Nina scrolled through the list of cars down to the F, where a handful of the supercars showed up. "And why do you even have so many of them?"

Cassandra pressed a button on the wall, opening up the enormous sliding doors of the garage. "Come on, you defended me so valiantly before. Don't get all judgmental now."

Nina shook her head. It still struck her as unfair that one woman could spend millions without breaking a sweat, while that money could last Nina a lifetime. Or, rather, it used to. Now that she tasted it, Nina became increasingly comfortable with Cassandra's lust for luxury. Wasn't that fact alone enough to justify it? Cassandra didn't hoard it all for herself—she shared it with Nina and the others.

The garage lit up as they entered, bathing a few dozen cars in blinding bright light. Leslie ensured they were all parked properly, well-maintained, and ready to go. Nina cackled when she saw her old rust bucket had received the same treatment—and much-needed cleaning.

"Have you ever been inside one of those?" She leaned against Cassandra and pointed at her car.

"They're all just cars, really." Cassandra put her arm around Nina. "I bought most of these for Leslie and the others."

"You seem to favor the Ferraris, though."

"My dad grew up loving them." Cassandra's embrace wavered for a moment. "We didn't spend enough time together, but he loved touring country roads with me."

"I'm sorry," Nina said, rubbing Cassandra's shoulder. "I didn't know."

Cassandra stopped and forced a smile. "I miss him, but his death made me realize we need to savor every moment we have on this planet."

"And not just on this planet, right?" Nina asked, recalling Jenny's comment about Cassandra's planned space adventure.

"What can I say to that?" Cassandra opened the passenger door of one of the convertible Ferraris. While it didn't have all the modern tricks of the Koenigsegg, it was a lot easier to get into with the roof down.

"You could say 'wanna come along?'," Nina said as she got in, testing the boundaries of her newfound wealth. Cassandra shook her head with a soft smile, saying sorry without speaking. There were limits, after all. Outer space appeared to be one of them. *Too bad.* Jenny's recent excitement about Star Trek had rubbed off on Nina. She could see herself floating in space with her billionaire girlfriend—having sex without gravity. *That'd be fun.*

The interior of the Ferrari screamed sports car, with red accents and fancy dials. A bright 'Start Engine' button on the steering wheel poked the beast to life, its howl bouncing off the garage walls.

With a mean grumble, the red convertible obeyed Nina's careful control as she steered it onto the main road. Like the Koenigsegg, it seemed to act before even thinking about touching the accelerator. The roar of the Ferrari and the way Cassandra's hair flowed in the wind almost made Nina forget about the egg inside her pussy. Almost.

Nina beamed when she caught Cassandra staring. Only the threat of the vibrator spinning to life in her pussy kept Nina from commenting. She got comfortable in the powerful supercar, her mind settling on the joyful knowledge that she had conquered Cassandra's heart.

NINA FELT LIKE THE RICH GIRL CASSANDRA WAS as she pulled up to the restaurant's parking lot. A bunch of guys stopped in their tracks to admire the car. They whistled when the Ferrari rolled past them, their comments muffled by the grumbling engine. Nina took her time in maneuvering the restless beast. She picked a spot she could drive straight out of when they came back. While the supercar seemed a lot more nimble than her old car, Nina didn't plan on reversing with an audience.

Cassandra used the remote to put the roof up after they got out. The three men came closer already, and one of them called out. Nina tensed up, uncomfortable at yet another confrontation, but Cassandra's hand on her shoulder offered a sense of protection.

"Yo, is that super fast?" The nearest guy asked. He wore a simple hoodie over a pair of jeans, the youthful style not matching his thirty-something age.

"Uh, I mean, it's not slow." Nina shrugged, chuckling at his weird choice of words as she tried to figure out what part of the car he stared at. Driving it offered a thrill, but she never understood the appeal of gawking at cars.

Cassandra nuzzled against Nina's neck. "*Superfast* is the name, dear."

Nina raised her eyebrows. "That's a dumb name. Especially when the Koenigsegg is super faster."

The excited middle-aged man snapped his head Nina's way when she mentioned the other exotic. "Holy shit, you have a Koenigsegg?"

Nina pointed at Cassandra with pride. "My girlfriend does."

"Damn," he said, rubbing his chin as he returned to admiring the red sports car, already losing interest in the women again.

"Oh, you think that's bad?" Cassandra spun Nina around and walked her to the restaurant. "They also made a Ferrari LaFerrari."

Nina snorted. "Bullshit."

"It's too silly to make up, isn't it?" Cassandra guided Nina past the host at the entrance, requiring no introduction.

"By now, I'm willing to believe anything," Nina said. After all, Cassandra turned her life upside down in ways she wouldn't have dared dream of. A waitress led the girls to a table at the far side, secluded from the rest. Nina snickered. *The plebs.* With the vibrator in her pussy, Nina welcomed every bit of privacy. As she recalled Cassandra's earlier taunts, Nina shivered. *This is going to be one hell of a first date.*

First Date

CHAPTER 13

Nina pulled back a chair for Cassandra before the waitress could. Cassandra sat down elegantly. In private, she showed a whole new side of her, but in public, she still played the role of uppity Miss Cardona. Still, she seemed a little less bratty than she had been with the barista when Nina first met her.

The smiling woman offered wine on the house, which Cassandra accepted with some formality. She could buy the whole place without thinking twice about it, but it was the thought that counted. *I guess.* Nina shrugged when the waitress left. "I bet dinner here is expensive enough that complimentary drinks should be mandatory."

Cassandra shook her head. "I'm insulted you assume everything I do is excessive."

Nina opened her mouth to comment, but she held back. She glanced around the restaurant. It didn't seem all that fancy. She raised her eyebrows at Cassandra, who frowned back. *What?*

Nina laughed when she saw the prices on the menu. This wasn't expensive at all—at least not by billionaire standards.

"Hope told me you loathe fancy dinners," Cassandra said. "So, here we are. Being normal."

Cassandra waved around her. "Jenny's parents run this place. It's really down to earth here, trust me."

Nina shook her head, speechless. Winning her heart sure made Cassandra more relaxed. It did nothing about the vibrator in her pussy, however, lying in wait for a command. Nina awaited the promised punishment with a raised pulse.

"So, tell me about yourself." Cassandra clasped her hands together. She couldn't hide her grin, and Nina's smile formed just by seeing her girlfriend happy.

"Well, I got a new job," Nina said, playing along. "Boss is a bit of a bitch, but the benefits are all right."

Nina grinned as she joked some more. She didn't catch Cassandra reaching for her phone to activate the vibrator. Nina yelped, covering her mouth while clenching her thighs together.

"Oh, fuck," she mumbled as the waitress glanced her way. Thankfully, the raven-haired woman moved on. Nina balled her fists. "Damn you..."

"What was that?" Cassandra cocked her head. The intensity of the toy increased. Her eyes lit up as Nina leaned forward, holding back a deep moan. Nina exhaled when the massage's strength lowered, glaring at her girlfriend.

"Don't give me that look," Cassandra said. When she lowered her finger toward her phone, Nina forced a cute smile.

"Better," Cassandra said. "You were telling me about your boss?"

Nina groaned but didn't respond, instead taking a look at the menu. She had to thank Hope later—it made a world of difference that Cassandra picked a simpler establishment. She couldn't stand those fancy places where they serve tiny courses all evening.

"Well, my boss is very kind and generous," Nina said. "She understands that showing mercy is the key to winning someone's heart."

Nina held her breath as Cassandra tapped the phone, but the sex toy's pulses remained steady inside her pussy. She sighed and thanked her lover, though the continuous, slow rumble of the toy alone had her all flustered.

"She sounds like an amazing woman," Cassandra said. She smiled at the waitress and said, "I'll have the ratatouille, my dear."

"Excellent choice." The lady bowed before turning to Nina with a questioning smile.

Nina glanced at Cassandra, whose finger hovered over her phone. The moment she tried to speak, the shifting rhythm of the toy in her pussy teased her. The vibrations peaked higher and became irregular, drawing a giggle from Nina's mouth.

"Miss?" The waitress leaned sideways a little to get Nina's attention, but the vibrator took priority. Nina adjusted in her seat, smiling with her lips pressed together. She felt sweat running down her back and forming at her brow. If she didn't speak now, it would only get worse.

"Grilled salmon," Nina said through her teeth. "Please."

While she tried to smirk to show more kindness than her hurried whispers indicated, Cassandra played around with the toy, keeping Nina struggling to stay still. The waitress masked any emotions behind a warm expression.

"Ooh," Nina cried out when the waitress walked away. She had to cover her mouth once more to stop everyone else from noticing. Her fancy makeup and dress could not compensate for her uneasy behavior. She reached under the table for just a moment, almost surrendering to her needs before pulling back.

"Everything all right, darling?" Cassandra asked, pretending she had nothing to do with Nina's excitement. "You seem a little bothered."

"Come on," Nina hissed. "That was rude toward the waitress."

"Yes, you were rude. Bad girl."

The vibrator worked randomly, sending little shocks through Nina's body. Little shocks that turned into persistent waves. She pressed her legs together under the table. *Damn you.*

"What was that?" Cassandra frowned while turning the intensity up. Nina clenched her teeth. *I didn't say that out loud, did I?* She held her hands against her belly, wanting nothing more than to send them lower and tend to her needs.

The waitress returned to interrupt them, asking Nina if she wanted lemon garlic or honey mustard sauce with her salmon.

"Yes," Nina mumbled. The server gave her a confused smile. *It's a decision, you idiot.* Nina looked away, holding her breath, but she failed to prevent a sharp 'ah!' from slipping out.

"Are you all right, miss?"

"Cramps," Nina said. "So sorry."

The waitress grunted an acknowledgement, still awaiting an answer. Nina raised her hand to her mouth. She hadn't even listened to the options. "Surprise me."

Feeling sorry for her awkward manners, Nina couldn't look the woman in the eye. She promised to apologize for it later, although she had no idea how.

"The honey mustard is delightful," the waitress said. Nina just smiled and nodded. *Yes, whatever.* As they were left alone again, she glared at her girlfriend.

"I can't handle this anymore," she said. "Let's go to the restroom. I'll eat you out the way you like?"

"Oh, pet," Cassandra waved dismissively, "this isn't about me. It's all about you, tonight."

Nina groaned. "Why do I even love you?"

"I asked you that before, didn't I?"

She recalled it all too well—the gut-wrenching conversation they had when they went for a ride. And yet, a day later, Nina conquered Cassandra's heart. As the memory of that victory distracted her, Cassandra tickled Nina's thighs with her toes.

"Fuck!" Nina blurted out. Nobody seemed to have heard—or they didn't care. She moved a hand under the table to force Cassandra away, but it became an awkward battle that she had no hopes of winning—not with the vibrator surging high and low inside her. She let go of Cassandra's foot, leaning back a little to surrender herself. It wouldn't take long, not like this. She closed her eyes, humming as Cassandra teased her thighs—and then her pussy. The nylon-clad toes wiggled along her labia. One of Nina's hands went down again to answer the irresistible urges in her pussy. She pouted when Cassandra pulled back and lowered the sex toy's setting way down.

"Oh, come on," Nina said. "I don't deserve this."

"Maybe." Cassandra held out her hand as she leaned forward. "But I have a surprise for you if you last until dessert."

Nina put her trembling, sweaty hand on Cassandra's. "I don't think I can."

Cassandra smiled as she caressed Nina. "Try."

She increased the toy's force right after. Nina squeezed Cassandra's hand hard. It wasn't just a spasm of her muscles—she wanted to punish her girlfriend as well. The cruel teasing had her riding toward a high that she feared would burst at the worst possible moment. *How much stronger can this thing go?*

Right as Nina doubted her resolve, the buzzing stopped. Cassandra patted her hand, giving her an unexpected break when their meals arrived. Nina thanked the waitress now that she could speak again.

"Hmm, I picked the right sauce," Nina said with a wink, hoping some lighthearted conversation would keep Cassandra's hands away from her phone. "I'm glad you didn't take me to one of those fancy-pants places."

Cassandra showed less poshness than Nina expected. No prim and proper etiquette—just two girlfriends having a normal dinner. Aside from Nina's flushed face and the toy inside her...or the fact she sat across a billionaire who chose her, of all people, as her partner. *Her housewife.* Nina beamed as she realized Cassandra provided everything she ever desired.

"That good, huh?" Cassandra nodded at the salmon.

Nina played the game right back at her and said, "Yes, you are."

THEY ENJOYED THEIR MEAL with light flirting and small talk, giving Nina enough time to cool down from the sexual teasing so she could enjoy her simple dinner in peace. It didn't stop her from tensing up when Cassandra put down her fork. Nina sighed when the fingers reached for the wineglass instead.

"So, what did you think of Hope's business plan?" Nina asked, forcing her mind away from the heat inside her.

"Oh, she's passionate about it, all right. So I've financed her endeavor."

"Cass…" Nina's shoulders slumped. The last thing she wanted was for her best friend to be in her girlfriend's debt—financial or otherwise.

"I didn't do it because she's your friend," Cassandra said. "Well, not only. I believe she'll pour her soul into it. Besides, what else am I gonna do? Buy another Ferrari?"

Nina groaned at the joke. "I'm sorry. I guess I'm still a bit weary of rich people, that's all."

"She said, wearing a ten-thousand-dollar dress."

"Very funny." Nina glanced at the dress. "Wait, really?"

Cassandra shrugged. "Worth it. You look delicious in it."

Nina sighed. Such conversations took getting used to. While the ease of spending for Cassandra clashed with her whole—previous—lifestyle, Nina reminded herself not to worry about Hope. If any-one knew how to stand up for themselves, it was Nina's best friend. And Cassandra didn't seem like the type to fret over a business investment—let alone hurt Nina's feelings.

"Thank you," Nina said. "For everything."

Cassandra's face lit up, but the server's return kept her from responding.

"Was the salmon to your liking?" The waitress smiled at Cassandra as she took the plates.

"Delicious," Nina said. "I'll be back for more!"

"We're delighted to have you anytime."

With Nina's lack of attention to Cassandra, the renewed stirring in her pussy came as a complete surprise. She slammed her hand on the table. Hoping to save grace, she played it off as excitement. "Excellent!"

Cassandra's laugh broke Nina's posture while the waitress treated the couple with undeserved respect. She bowed before leaving them without so much as a frown.

Nina glared at Cassandra, earning her a rougher treatment of the toy. The rhythm became more ran-dom, with intense ups and drawn-out downs. Nina rubbed herself under the table, unable to resist her heat, even as Cassandra clicked her tongue.

"Please," Nina whispered. "Before she comes back."

Cassandra didn't give her the release she craved. As Nina got closer to losing herself, Cassandra tuned the toy's settings to tease more and more and or-dered Nina to hold her hands above the table. Nina obeyed, fighting her desires. Her nipples stiffened so much that she glanced down to confirm what she feared—they pressed visibly against her glittery dress.

"So slutty." Cassandra sipped her wine. "I'm not sure such a wanton girl is the right one for me."

Nina wanted to respond, yet no words came out of her mouth—just a slight moan as the toy rumbled in waves. She bit her lip and cupped her tits, ignoring Cassandra's shushing. *I'm almost there...*

Once again, the waitress interrupted her attempts to surrender to climax. Nina's hands shot back onto the table, pressing flat on the surface in a way that wasn't relaxed or normal.

"Dessert, ladies?" The server handed them another menu. Nina saw the text on the paper but couldn't focus on any of the words. The never-ending pleasure ebbing and flowing from her pussy made her a little dizzy while she wiggled around. She agreed to the same ice cream Cassandra chose so she didn't have to speak as much.

The moment the waitress stepped away, Nina played with her tits again, shamelessly tweaking her nipples as she whimpered. She no longer cared about getting caught—that would be Cassandra's mess to clean up. Nina just wanted to get off. She ignored Cassandra's disapproving scowl.

"Nini, stop," Cassandra hissed. But Nina didn't stop. Not until Cassandra shut the toy down. Nina groaned at the sudden peace in her pussy, even if it did nothing to lower her needs—the lack of stimulation was its own stimulation.

"You said if I lasted until dessert," Nina whispered. "Not *through* dessert."

She glanced at the door leading to the kitchen and fingered herself without permission. Cassandra put her hand on the table again, with her palm up. "Fine. Hold my hand and close your eyes."

Surprised at Cassandra's mercy, Nina stopped playing with herself to do as she was told. She took Cassandra's hand and closed her eyes, panting in anticipation. The vibrating returned in slow, gentle waves while the corners of Nina's lips curled in the same rhythm. Her surroundings disappeared. She kept her eyes closed when Cassandra urged her to, even as the waitress put the ice cream down in front of her. The server's presence no longer bothered her.

"Nina." Cassandra squeezed her hand. A moan slipped out just from hearing Cassandra whisper her name. She rose with every wave inside her pussy, then sank back when it lowered, following the rhythm. It became almost trance-like. The pace increased. Nina hummed. Cassandra told her to keep her eyes closed. Cold metal touched the tip of one of her fingers, but it came second to the tingling in Nina's core. She tensed up. *So close.* Cassandra chuckled as she slid the ring down Nina's finger. *Wait. A ring?* Nina's heart skipped a beat when her eyes shot open. She stared right at the prettiest diamond ring she had ever seen.

"Marry me," Cassandra said.

Nina gasped. Cried. Shrieked. Her eyes darted from the glittering ring on her finger to Cassandra's doe eyes. She clenched her hand around her girlfriend's. *Yes.* She whispered it. She shouted it. "YES!"

Nina's thighs bucked and her heart fluttered. She didn't fight her climax, whimpering as tears ran down her cheeks. "Oh, Cass. Yes...fuck yes!"

"Are you sure?" Cassandra beamed at Nina. Her eyes were watery, too. Nina grasped Cassandra's hands and leaned over the table, her body trembling. They met halfway to kiss each other, careless about anything else in the world. Nina just about crawled onto the table to embrace her girlfriend—her *fiancée*. She smooched Cassandra's lips, cheeks, and nose. "Oh, Cass…"

NINA STARED AT THE DIAMOND on the thin ring. She had been staring at it for a minute now. Or two. Maybe five. Cassandra somehow finished her dessert, but Nina's belly filled with jittery butterflies instead. She gawked at her lover. "I don't know what to say."

"Too late!" Cassandra's smile had never been so pronounced. "You already said yes."

Nina giggled as she took her fiancée's hands. She caressed Cassandra's fingers and looked her in the eyes.

"My heart is still racing," Nina said. "It will never beat the same again."

"Come here." Cassandra urged Nina around the table and made her put her hand on Cassandra's chest. "My pulse is through the roof. I was so anxious."

Nina cocked her head. "You? Why?"

"I was afraid you might say no…"

Cassandra's voice cracked, and Nina held back a joke. She kissed her lover. Her girlfriend. Her soon-to-be wife. The vulnerability showed as Nina hugged Cassandra close.

"I'm glad you asked, anyway," Nina said. "I don't think I would've been so brave."

Cassandra nuzzled her face against Nina's. They hugged each other tight, and the waitress gave them some space. Nina giggled and pulled back. "Cassandra?"

"Hmm?"

"Do you realize what you've done?" Nina tried to sound as serious as possible while wiping away a tear of joy. Going by Cassandra's uncertain frown, it worked. Nina tapped her fiancée on the nose. "You literally proposed on the first date."

Space Sex

EPILOGUE

SIX MONTHS LATER

Nina just finished making breakfast for her wife, a ritual she stuck to wherever they went. She held the burrito with both hands, ensuring everything stayed together. Back home, dropping a pepper or egg mattered little—she could just kneel and pick it up. Things were trickier in space, where anything she dropped ended up drifting around. Nina braced her foot against the wall of the *Scimitar*, their cozy spacecraft, then pushed herself away to float toward Cassandra.

Nina's wife stared outside through the dome, her gorgeous brown hair tied in a neat bun. Though the dark jumpsuit lacked the sexiness of the billionaire's usual luxury wear, she still looked amazing in it. She leaned against the edge of the cupola, gazing at the world below with her bare feet dangling in the air.

Nina's ponytail trailed behind her as she approached her beloved—and crashed into her.

"Oopsie." Nina squeezed the burrito as she collided with Cassandra, sending the two of them drifting into the window. Pieces of eggs, bacon, and onions went their own way, the lack of gravity scattering bits of the meal around them. Cassandra inched away to snatch some of it with her fingers, ending up sideways in relation to Nina. They chased the floating chaos, giggling and flicking the chunks of breakfast at one another.

"I don't think we're supposed to make such a mess," Cassandra said. She hung upside down, snatching half the burrito Nina threw her way.

"Too bad." Nina watched an onion pass her by. "Because we'll be making a much bigger mess in a minute."

She had planned on making love to her wife the moment they got into space, but the launch day had exhausted both of them. With long hours of preparation and the stress of being launched out of the Earth's atmosphere on a huge rocket, Nina hadn't the strength to try it last night. Instead, they had stared at the planet below them for two hours—long enough to go around the Earth—before falling asleep in each other's arms.

"You know, I paid many millions so you could see our planet from above," Cassandra said as she drifted about. "If I knew you were just going to gawk at me eat, we could've gone camping instead."

Nina shook her head, her ponytail snaking around her face. "It's not my fault you're so beautiful."

She told Cassandra that she had slept for maybe four hours tops, spending the rest of the time cuddling her wife and gazing at the big blue planet. Night and day were going to be a strange concept for the next forty-eight hours. While Cassandra had snored in Nina's arms, the *Scimitar* orbited the Earth three times. Nina couldn't get enough of it—crossing continents and oceans within minutes. But she also couldn't get enough of Cassandra's smile.

"I have to admit something, though," Nina said.

Cassandra frowned as she finished her burrito. "What's that?"

Nina fought back a grin. She tried to sound serious when she said, "you're no longer the prettiest girl on the planet."

Though Cassandra rolled her eyes, the smirk on her face matched Nina's. They hadn't stopped smiling from the moment the crew helped them into their suits the day before.

"That's okay." Cassandra pushed herself away from the chair, toward Nina. "I don't think I'm...attracted to you anymore."

Nina snorted as she caught her wife in her arms. They drifted backward against the dome while Cassandra's lips brushed Nina's cheek.

"I love you so fucking much." Cassandra kissed Nina's neck, nuzzling against her.

"Prove it." Nina pressed down on Cassandra's head and threw her legs around her wife's waist.

Nina smiled while trying to remain still. Cassandra tugged the zipper of the blue jumpsuit, kissing Nina's bare skin as she exposed more of it. She hummed in appreciation when she unclasped Nina's simple black bra.

"They look bigger," Cassandra whispered. She squeezed one of Nina's tits and peppered it with kisses. Nina held on to Cassandra to keep her from drifting away, the flapping of her wife's feet having no effect in space.

"And you look cuter." Nina stroked Cassandra's face. "Like a space mermaid."

With Cassandra struggling to lower the zipper of Nina's suit further, they pushed and pulled, trying to get into a better position to strip one another out of the unflattering outfits. After a minute of nudging, Nina shoved her wife back to undress herself instead. She smirked at Cassandra, who slowly tumbled around with nothing to grab.

"Uh…" Cassandra's hands clawed at nothing as she rolled along in the air. "This is new."

Nina laughed at the sight of Cassandra trying to swim in space while twirling around her core. It gave Nina enough of a break to slip her suit down her body. She had figured out how to stay in place—by tucking her feet behind a luggage net. Once she got out of her attire, she flicked the floating suit at her wife and put one foot under the thick straps again.

Cassandra grabbed her seat when she got in range of it, working her legs under the seatbelt so she, too, could strip. Nina licked her lips when Cassandra took off the simple thong—then tossed it her way. She leaned to the side to catch the floating panties on her face, snatching them with her mouth.

"Do you like how my pussy tastes?" Cassandra dipped a finger in her pussy, then licked it clean. "I know I do."

Nina sucked on the fabric for a bit. "That's such a vain thing to say."

"Can you blame me?"

Nina shrugged. *Not really.* She beckoned her wife while getting rid of her panties as well. Cassandra dove back in, drifting closer until she bumped into the bags at Nina's feet. She kissed all over Nina's toes, soles, and calves, proving her affection on every inch of her skin. Once more, Cassandra's jerky movements made her twist and turn in zero gravity, holding on to Nina's legs to keep close.

"Stay still," Cassandra said, giggling as she climbed back up to kiss Nina. "Come here, damn it."

"You're the one swimming backward." Nina tapped her wife on the nose. "And your kicking isn't doing anything."

Cassandra grunted, her neck craned to meet Nina's lips from her sideways floating position.

"Hold on." Nina grabbed Cassandra's shoulders to flip her around until they faced each other upside down. "Now you can go down in a sixty-nine."

Cassandra smooched Nina before following her lead. "You mean, go up."

"Shut up." Nina pulled Cassandra down—or up —by her sides to put her face right where she wanted it. Without hesitation or teasing, Cassandra lapped at Nina's slit while pulling herself into an up-side-down embrace, working her face between Nina's thighs.

"Oh, eager, are we?" Nina took Cassandra's head with one hand. Her toned thighs hugged Cassandra's face, squeezing her lover. She held her wife by her ass, keeping her from floating away again.

"Lick me," Cassandra cooed. She moved her legs onto Nina's shoulders and behind her head, pulling Nina's mouth right against her pussy. Nina dove in, copying her lover's motions, smooching Cassandra's labia. Her wife's devotion turned needy, sucking on her clit without warning. She yelped as the muscles in her belly tensed, Cassandra's sudden roughness driving her wild.

With only one foot holding herself steady, Nina floated forward, sending the lovers into a slow spin.

She didn't stop it, finding it more important to hold Cassandra's face down—and to keep her mouth on her wife's lovely pussy. She unhooked her foot from the net to clench Cassandra's head between her thighs.

Floating together, Nina and Cassandra kissed each other's pussies with lewd smacks. They twirled around, bumping into the walls, chairs, and window. Nina wiggled her tongue between her lover's lips, sinking deep to satisfy her lover like she had done so many times before. She thought back to the day they met. When she still feared Cassandra. Her heart fluttered at the memory of it—of Cassandra's mean face. They replayed the event from time to time, drawing on Nina's submissiveness in restrooms, elevators, and anywhere else they found a risky moment to fuck.

Cassandra knew how to tease, breaking away from Nina's throbbing clit when her high neared. She lapped Nina's labia, delaying her orgasm while keeping her close to the edge. Nina tried to pay back in kind, but Cassandra's stronger thighs held on tight, preventing Nina from doing anything but French kiss her pussy.

Nina adored going down on Cassandra, swooning at the massaging muscles of her wife's vagina. Her tongue never failed to satisfy Cassandra, and she recognized the impending high.

Cassandra rewarded Nina's deep kisses by returning her mouth to Nina's clit, ever aggressive in the way she sucked, kissed, and licked. Nina gasped as her lover took her throbbing clit between her lips and flicked the very tip of her tongue over her button, the frantic movements sending her over the edge.

Nina whimpered into Cassandra's pussy, still tongue fucking her wife. She grabbed Cassandra's head with both hands to hold her down, while Cassandra's thighs clamped down around Nina's face, smothering each other with their pussies. Nina's body jerked, her belly tightening as Cassandra moaned on her clit. They bounced off the floor and crashed against the walls, their muscles locked in a shuddering embrace of lust. Nina withdrew her tongue from Cassandra only when her lungs burned so much she feared damaging herself, while Cassandra kissed Nina's pussy a little more. They ended up with their naked, sweaty bodies against the window, panting and giggling.

NINA PULLED CASSANDRA INTO HER ARMS. They would have to deal with the muskiness of their sweaty love for another two days. She didn't mind. Neither did Cassandra, based on her wide smile. If anything, Nina yearned to repeat it.

"That was something," Cassandra said as Nina kissed her nose. "I'm pretty sure I have bruises from all that banging around."

"Well, you almost broke my neck with your thighs." Nina took Cassandra's hands. "Not that I would mind going out like that."

She rubbed her thumb over Cassandra's wedding ring while they floated about, hands held and ankles crossed.

Nina cupped Cassandra's chin and gazed into her eyes. "Can we stay here forever?"

She knew the answer to that silly question, but she wanted to remain in the moment forever. Nina couldn't look away from the doe eyes of her wife. As bratty as Cassandra once appeared to her, Nina only saw pure adoration.

They hadn't been the same since the day Cassandra confessed her love. Nina's pride had grown, along with some arrogance. She never lowered her head anymore. She didn't doubt herself, let alone her relationship. Together, they were whole. Cassandra bolstered Nina's confidence, while Nina filled her wife's heart with the one thing money couldn't buy. *Love.*

Nina nuzzled against Cassandra's cheek, their mutual love larger than the blue Earth they gazed at.

THE END

FREE STORY & NEWSLETTER

Sign up for my newsletter to get to know me a little better...and receive a spicy short story!

In *Stuck Going Down*, Makayla and her kinky neighbor Kylie get trapped in the tiny, old elevator of their apartment building.
With the mechanic still hours away, Kylie puts the shy lesbian in her place once and for all.
But Makayla enjoys being dominated, and there is no line she won't cross for her hot and mean neighbor.

The story is a little too STEAMY for Amazon.

ABOUT
CLAIRE KIRKLAND

Growing up, I struggled with my feelings toward powerful women. The bullies in college, a rival co-worker, or my demanding boss. I envied them. Hated them. It took years before I realized I wanted to *worship* them. The rude awakening filled my head with crazy desires. Some are a little risky, others downright unprofessional. But when a stern domme narrows her eyes, my legs go weak. I can't help it!

Now, I write about (not so) innocent lesbians finding pleasure in submitting to strong women…even if some need a little guidance.

When I'm not writing—or getting stepped on—I love to go out for long walks through nature, sometimes on the back of a horse. At night, I often gaze at the night sky, wondering what—and who—else is out there in the endless sea of stars.